THE WRONG SIDE OF SUNDOWN

SUNSET STATION
BOOK 1

GENE DOUCETTE

The Wrong Side of Sundown

Cover by Kim Killion

KRIS

THERE WERE twelve decently expensive rectangles in a non-geostationary orbit above the Earth. The rectangles were composed of a metal alloy that was both strong and lightweight, with the former being an especially important feature for an object expected to survive in space, and the latter especially important when trying to get it *into* space.

Each of the twelve rectangles was precisely ten feet long, five feet wide, and nine inches thick. They were connected to one another—thanks to screws composed of the same metal alloy that fit neatly into predrilled holes—making one much larger rectangle, measuring thirty feet long and twenty feet wide.

One of the reasons these rectangles were decently expensive was due to their location, i.e., in space, which is difficult (and costly) to get to. Another was that there was an embedded propulsion lattice on the bottom of each rectangle. (With "bottom" being defined here as, "the side facing the Earth.") This propulsion lattice kept the rectangles—individually and collectively—from falling out of orbit, which is a thing that doesn't seem like it could happen upon reaching a certain altitude, but which very much could.

The top of each rectangle had an outer layer of ferromagnetic metal. This was so the rectangles, once joined by many, many more of their fellow rectangles, could serve as a platform on which people with magnetic boots might walk. This layer added both weight and expense, but without it, the rectangles couldn't serve their intended function: as pieces of an orbiting space platform.

There was a thirteenth decently expensive rectangle that was also in orbit, very near the other twelve. It was supposed to attach to the side of rectangles one and two, vertically to their horizontal. Like the others, it had a propulsion lattice, a magnetic layer, and predrilled holes for screws.

Unlike the other twelve, number thirteen's holes adamantly refused to line up.

"No, stop, no, come back," Kris said, as she watched a screw float just out of her reach.

Kris's comms link chirped. *"How can I be of assistance?"* Susie asked.

"Shut up, asshat," Kris said.

"Of course!" Susie said.

"You shouldn't call her that, dear," Davina said, from inside the shuttle. "Not on an open channel. Is there a problem?"

"The new panel doesn't fit, for some reason," Kris said. "I think I need to get the drill. Also, I'm now short a screw. It's on its way to... what is that, the South China Sea?"

"Do you need help? I can get Paul up if you're jammed."

"I shouldn't *need* the drill is really the point, Dav," Kris said. "It should fit. No, don't wake him."

Davina—along with Paul, who was on his sleep shift—was in the shuttle. It was parked a little more than two thousand feet away, which wasn't *that* far, but given how long it would take to,

1: wake up Paul and, 2: get him to suit up. to, 3: get outside and help, he may as well be on the surface. And Davina couldn't suit up herself without waking Paul first; someone had to be awake and at the controls.

Kris also didn't necessarily need help; the drill was in the toolkit attached to the magnetic side of the space platform. She just needed to let go of panel thirteen first—according to the pertinent laws of physics governing this circumstance, it *should* stay more or less where it was—swap out the power screwdriver for the power drill, and adjust the holes so that they lined up with the holes on rectangles one and two. Then, she could swap power tools again, finish attaching rectangle thirteen, go back to the shuttle, and call it a day.

All doable, except one of the screws was currently floating away—governed by a different clause in the same physical law that was keeping rectangle thirteen in place—and they didn't think to send up any extras.

"Kris, this is mission control," Morris said, barging in on Dav and Kris's channel. "Sounds like you've got something going on up there. How can we help? Also, stop calling Susie that."

Morris was one of the roughly seventeen team members at the Monterrey mission control whose entire, full-time existence, was keeping the shuttle crew alive. They were good at it, but even if they weren't, Kris and her team would probably still have to be somewhat nice to them, because they were also the people who sent unmanned shuttles with food, water, and oxygen up to the station. "Don't mess with the supply chain," was one of Kris's governing principles.

At the same time, Morris was pissing her off, and that simply had to be addressed.

"Really?" Kris said. "This is your first thought? I'm not giving an interview here; you guys are the only ones who can hear me."

"You're on a live feed to the entire control room, Krista," Morris said. "Something like half of Monterrey heard you. What if there was a school tour?"

Mo was in charge of the aforementioned seventeen person team, and in his role as supervisor, he occasionally used full names as a means to express his displeasure. It was possible he didn't know he did this.

"Okay, okay," Kris said. "I'll watch my language. Can we move on, please?"

"We can," he said. "What's going on?"

"Well, Mo? I'm on hour eight of this walk, and the IKEA furniture you sent up here doesn't fit. So now I have to re-drill the holes, except I'm down a screw, because in the process of my *trying* to get the goddamn thing to fit, the screw decided to go on a tour of Southeast Asia. Since I don't want to be out here another ten hours because you guys can't take proper measurements, I'm about ready to shove this asshole panel into the ionosphere, and then maybe do the same with the other five panels back at the ESS. Now, go ahead and tell me how you can help."

After a pause, Morris said, "Standby. We'll get back to you."

There was a gentle click that indicated they were no longer being heard by mission control.

"Tactful," Davina said.

"Babe, I ran out of tact an hour ago," Kris said.

"*The time is, thirteen hundred and seven, Monterrey local,*" Susie said cheerfully.

"I said shut up, asshat," Kris said.

"*Of course!*" Susie said.

WHEN THE TEAM at Ellis Aerospace first introduced Susie, she was called the Asset Support Bot, where "asset" was the preferred pronunciation of the acronym AAST, which stood for Augmented Aerospace Science and Technology. In coming up with what her creators no doubt thought was a clever acronym, they failed to think through how the people working with their support bot might elect to manipulate this naming convention.

Specifically—and Kris was definitely not the only person to do this—when one added the small "a" from "Science *and* Technology" to the acronym, one got AASaT, which is hard to read as anything other than "asshat".

It was no coincidence that, a few months after the Asset Support Bot rolled out, she was rebranded as Susie the Support Bot. This did not stop anyone who had been calling her "asshat" from continuing to do so, although this may have been because nobody liked Susie.

Susie the Support Bot was by *far* the most famous member of the Ellis Aero team. This was more or less completely the fault of the company's founder, Max Ellis, who in his entire life had never missed a promotional opportunity.

In addition to privately funding and partially realizing the creation of the world's first reusable space platform, Max—through his company Ellis Intelligence—developed specialized artificial intelligence "bots" for use in just about any product that ran on electricity.

He called them bots, because he wanted users to imagine that they were dealing with a robot who existed physically somewhere, which *seemed* stupid, until the design team (from Ellis Design) rolled out realistic-looking "photos" of the actual bots, complete with names, preferred pronouns, and accessories. Nobody cared that the supposed photos were the product of a group—Ellis Arts—that specialized in deepfake images; it was somehow easier for consumers to interact with their talking toaster, if they thought the toaster was being operated remotely by a bot named Margaret, who was partial to blue eye shadow and liked sunsets.

Susie the Support Bot was supposed to be, literally, one of the team. According to Ellis Aero, everything Kris and the rest of the humans did was vetted and/or *ordered* by Susie... as if *she* was actually the one in charge. Susie was supposedly the ultimate problem-solving crewmate, the one who never slept and always had an eye on everything, was poised to issue life-saving commands, prevent terrible things from happening before they happened, and even dole out advice to any depressed and/or suicidal humans.

Much of this misinformation was promulgated via an online series of dramatic vignettes, wherein different supposed real-life crises were reenacted, and kind, smart Susie saved the day. There was also a line of children's books, and rumors of an upcoming videogame.

Susie was, very much by design, a media star.

What made all of it especially annoying was that the actual Susie the Support Bot was about as useful as an online search engine; she wasn't *real* AI, in the true sense of the term, i.e., an independent intelligence created artificially. (Non-trivially, this was true of all AI created by Ellis Intelligence, but that was a conversation for another time.) All Susie could do was parrot basic facts, usually at inconvenient times, at someone who already knew those basic facts.

Susie's actual work—rather, the work the media gave her credit for—was being done by a team of humans on the planet, or by the people in space that the support bot was supposed to be supporting. But anytime Kris or one of her teammates spoke *to* the public, they had to credit Susie for things she absolutely did not do.

With all that in mind, it was kind of amazing that, "Commander Krista Standard called Susie the Support Bot an 'asshat' on a national broadcast" was the worst headline the Ellis people could fathom. Because Kris—and pretty much everyone else on the mission—was one more useless suggestion away from unplugging Susie.

They just had to figure out how to do that.

———

KRIS WAS BONE-TIRED, and unsustainably damp. Underneath the bulky spacesuit, she had on a skintight bodysuit that was supposed to keep her body temperature at an acceptable level. Arguably, it did not work, although she'd never done a spacewalk without it, and so couldn't attest to what *that* would be like; for all she knew, it was doing a brilliant job under exigent circumstance. However, the fact remained that underneath the skintight bodysuit there was a sheen of sweat that had nowhere to go.

She'd been trying to work out a design solution to the problem. Her first idea was to find a way to evaporate the sweat and release it into space. But there was basically no way to emit a gas in zero gravity without it acting as a propellant, and that would definitely be bad. She considered collecting the evaporated sweat in a container instead, cooling it down, and dropping it off in the shuttle after the walk. But every model she drew up resulted in a miniature weather system inside the suit. Which would also definitely be bad.

She sighed, and turned slightly, to taken in an unobstructed view of Earth.

It was probably the most breathtaking view any human ever had the privilege of witnessing, and every time she took a moment for it, she told herself she definitely shouldn't take it for granted. This didn't work; she definitely *did* take it for granted.

Also, it wasn't *that* terrific, not compared to what it could have been.

They were in an orbit where the planet spun beneath them, while they remained in a comparatively fixed position. The sun was always up, shining on her left and hitting roughly half the planet. But thanks to where they were positioned, Kris didn't get to see very much of the lit side of the surface. She got roughly $1/5^{th}$ of it; the rest of the planet beneath her was currently experiencing nighttime. Sure, she could see the city lights and whatnot, but that wasn't the same as the big daytime view.

Floating in space on the wrong side of sundown, she thought.

It wasn't supposed to be like this. When Max Ellis recruited her from the NASA moon program, it was with the implicit understanding that she would be breaking *new* ground, making important *new* discoveries, etc.

"You will be at the vanguard of a new chapter in space," was how Max put it. The line was definitely written for him by someone on his public relations team, (she heard it again six month later—albeit in Spanish—in a recruitment ad for the Monterrey ground crew) but it hooked her all the same. Which was how a good P.R. pitch is supposed to work.

She *was* something of a trailblazer, as the youngest commander of her gender, which was nice, but not as important to her as the other point: with Ellis Aero, she would get to be *in* space much sooner than would have been possible at NASA.

This was because NASA was taking absolutely forever to get their moon program going. Here it was, three years after Kris decided to jump over to Ellis, and they *still* weren't on the moon, or even in lower orbit. In that regard, Kris had made the right choice.

Still, this wasn't at all what she had been promised. She was coming up on her tenth month off-planet, and it was clear that there would be no more new ground to break, because "new grounds" wasn't actually the job. The job was: road construction.

She turned around again, away from the planet view, until she was facing deep space.

The shuttle holding Davina and Paul was floating nearby; Kris could see Davina in the dome window, at the controls, looking bored, albeit a cute kind of bored. They had all lost weight in their time off-planet—Paul called the look, "consumption chic," which was horrible but not wrong—but on Davina it was more obvious than with anyone else. Dav had been a wisp of a girl when she joined up, to the extent that Kris was surprised she ever passed the physical requirements. Now it looked like she was barely there.

It was a small shuttle; three people was the max. And it was only for use *in* space, meaning if they steered it into the planet, they would all die sometime before reaching the thermosphere. When it wasn't out on a campaign—attaching new panels was the current campaign—it lived in a dock in the hub of the Ellis Space Station.

The three objects—the space station, the shuttle, and the nascent space platform—existed in a region of space that was called, collectively, Sunset Station. It was an optimistic title; it presumed the existence of more objects in the future, taking up more of the same region of space. Someday, perhaps, that would come true, but it was beginning to look like that wouldn't be happening in any of their lifetimes.

The ESS was some distance away, behind the shuttle. From Kris's angle, it looked like a badly designed propeller, with a large, square chamber at the end of a collapsible tunnel, spinning around an axis—the hub—offset on the other side by a metal box of equivalent mass, on a cable that extended only half the distance from the axis.

The spin approximated Earth gravity for anyone inside the

square chamber, which was formally called the Habitat. Informally, it was called—by members of the Ellis Aerospace P.R. team (who—importantly—never had to live inside of it) Tahiti. Informally, by the people who actually had to *live* there, it was called the bucket.

In another two weeks, the bucket team of Alan, Josip and Sandee would rotate in, and Kris, Davina and Paul would rotate out, for their own six weeks in there.

The bucket was Ellis's solution to anyone spending too much time in space.

There was a host of medical reasons why nobody should be living off-planet for anything longer than two or three months. Primary among them was that nearly everything about being human revolved around existing in a constant 1G environment: bone growth, digestion, muscle maintenance, circulatory health, and on, and on. (Hence, the drastic weight loss.) But it was expensive to keep bringing people to the station, taking other people down from the station, training new people to go up, and so on. Better to keep a stable team in space for a length of time not exceeding a variable that used to be eighteen months but was now *Catch-22*-ing toward thirty-six months, and have them "recover" from the rigor of space by spending half of their time in a spinning hellbox that simulated normal gravity.

There was almost no scientific rigor behind the spinning bucket solution, as regards the deleterious effects on humans to long-term zero-gravity exposure. But that didn't stop Max Ellis, and a whole bunch of other people, from claiming they had resolved the problem.

⌈▭⌉

"WONDER WHAT WE'RE WAITING FOR," Davina said, at around the six minute mark.

"Don't know," Kris said. "Not sure there's a solution for, 'thing is wrong size.' Think they'd be pissed if I pushed it toward the horizon?"

"I don't think they'd be *happy*."

"*How can I help?*" Susie asked.

"Well, Susie," Kris said, "the problem is, the new panel is about a quarter of an inch too short. Do you have a solution for that?"

"*I don't understand the question!*" Susie said, enthusiastically. "*Can you rephrase?*"

"No. Be quiet."

"*Of course!*"

"Hey guys," Alan said, from the bucket. "We've been listening in. We were wondering if it could be attached cleanly in a different formation."

Alan was the only other member of the current six-person team who'd been recruited directly from NASA. Like Kris, he had experience working within a system that functioned somewhat better than whatever the hell Ellis Aero had going on. Davina, Paul and Sandee had been recruited directly from academia; their experience with systemic efficiency varied accordingly.

"Do you mean, attach it the long way and create a seventh row?" she asked. "Or attach it the short way and create a third horizontal row?"

"Either," Josip said. "I am wondering if *all* the panels have this problem, and the matter is that we never actually tried connecting them horizontal-to-vertical before."

Josip's resumé was better than anyone else's, because unlike the rest of them, he'd been to space before. A few years back, the European Space Agency funded a program whose intention was similar to the one currently being executed (badly) by Ellis Aerospace. Shortly after their success in launching what they called the Progress Capsule—an ostensibly permanent orbiting station—conflicting political interests spawned a crisis in funding, and the project was shut down. The crew, of which Josip was a member, only lasted two weeks before returning to the surface.

The Progress Capsule was still in a geosynchronous orbit; Josip used to hum the Polish national anthem every time it came past. Eventually, someone told him that was annoying, and he stopped.

"I guess we could try," Kris said, "but I'll need another set of hands if I want to move it again; I'm too spent to do this alone."

This wasn't, strictly speaking, because of the *weight* of the panel; it *had* no weight. But it had mass, and it had sharp corners. Moving it around without causing harm to herself meant going slowly and deliberately, and she didn't have enough in the tank for slow and deliberate.

"I can wake Paul," Davina said. "He can sub in."

"Maybe," Kris said, as her comms fluttered, indicating the ground had returned. "Let's hear what they say first."

"Kris, how are you doing?" Morris asked.

"I don't think you really want me to answer that, Mo," she said.

"Fair enough," he said. "So, um, we went back to the design team, and they reached out to the manufacturer. We have to run a couple of tests down here, but this is what we think happened. This new batch of panels from a different fabrication company than the other twelve; we're thinking the materials they used reacted differently, during payload delivery, than the original set. But what they're telling us that once the panel is seasoned, it should line up."

"Did you say, 'seasoned,' ground?" Davina asked. "This is not a piece of wood, or a frying pan."

"Morris," Kris said, "if I understand correctly... You're

saying they didn't account for the escape velocity G's when they made this panel. Is that right?"

"They *did* account for it," he said. "The specs are identical. But the metals were differently sourced."

"They went with a lower bidder," Alan said.

"That isn't what I said," Morris said.

"*Sounds* like that's what you're saying," Davina said.

"Morris," Alan said, "something actionable would be nice. Kris is on overtime."

"Yeah, ground, what do you want me to do here?" Kris asked. "Wait for this thing to grow a quarter inch?"

"That's affirmative," Morris said. "We believe it will expand to the correct dimensions in time."

"Yeah, that's... that sounds like bullshit, Mo," Kris said. "And it still doesn't solve the immediate problem, which is that it doesn't fit right *now*."

"We want you to bring it back inside, until it's ready to go," Morris said.

Kris sighed. "Susie," she said, "mute ground."

"*Muted*," Susie said.

(This was literally the only thing Susie was good for.)

"Guys, pushing it into the atmosphere's looking pretty promising right now," Kris said.

"Agreed," Davina said.

"I'm going to tell the ground to bite me. How's everyone feeling about that?"

"You are the commander," Josip said. "You speak for all of us. I think what you mean to say is that we, as a team, are telling the ground to bite us collectively. And we are okay with that."

"Same," Davina said, "but be nice."

"I'll try," Kris said. "Susie, unmute."

"*Unmuted*."

"Ground, are you there?" Kris asked.

"You know we can override the mute if we want," Morris said. He sounded annoyed, but he always did when he got muted.

"I do, but I assume you didn't listen in, because you want to keep us nice and happy, and buying into the illusion that we're allowed to have a minute of privacy in our lives," Kris said. "Here's the thing: it took over eight hours to get this panel into position, and it'll probably take at least four to put it back in the shuttle cargo hold again. You get that, right?"

"I get it, Kris," Morris said. "I'm only telling you what I've been told. I know it sucks."

Morris was actually a decent, reasonable guy, in no small part because he was also a member of the astronaut corps. If all went well, *he'd* be the one off-planet in eighteen months, cursing Susie and disobeying the more asinine orders, while Kris gave him those orders from the Monterrey control room.

She liked him. But there was a limit.

"Uh-huh, okay, here's what's going to happen, Mo," she said. "First, I'm gonna line up one hole and one slot, put a screw through it, and leave it where it is, for however long it takes for your little panel to grow up into a big panel. Then, I'm gonna head back to the hub and sleep for a week. When I wake up again, you can go ahead and tell me what the higher-ups think of my choice."

"Kris, if you do that..."

"If I *do* that, we'll have to go on another spacewalk with a tape measure or whatever. I know. I can also let it just float out here and we can take bets on how long before a piece of space debris, or a cosmic ray with a hard-on, bumps it into a new orbit. Either way, as mission commander, I am making the decision to put the safety of the crew—which, today, is *me*—ahead of the completion of the task. If they don't like that, they know where to find me. Susie, mute ground."

"Muted."

━━

IF YOU WENT by the information coming out of the public relations arm of the Ellis corporate conglomerate, the space platform was currently four times larger than it was in reality, and already had a roof on it. Also, if about three quarters of the artistic renditions were to be taken at face value, Sunset Station had already solved the artificial gravity problem.

There were three "photographs" on the internet that supposedly showed astronauts Davina Tombe and Alan Blanken walking along the platform without helmets, and *with* gravity. The photos were pretty terrific: grainy, a little out-of-focus, taken from a peculiar angle, as if captured surreptitiously and smuggled out of Ellis Aerospace at great personal risk. (What risk? That was unimportant.) They were good fakes, *so* good that some of the people who should know better were arguing that the "they're a fake" argument was disinformation put out by Ellis Aero, and that the *truth* was that the people at Ellis actually did have artificial gravity, but were keeping the technology secret.

The *actual* truth was that Ellis had created the photos themselves, as a viral promotional gimmick to bring attention to their space platform, and the science they hoped Sunset Station would be introducing to the world someday. But even when the Ellis team directly responsible for creating the fake photographs came right out and said so, almost nobody believed them.

The problem with all that reality-bending P.R. was that while it unquestionably brought more investors into Ellis Aerospace—which meant additional funds to build more, faster—hardly anyone on the ground knew how incredibly unpleasant it was to be in space for this long, and how far away they were from having a completed space platform… never mind one with walls and a ceiling, artificial gravity (which, again, hadn't even been cracked yet) and an atmosphere.

It should have been true that everyone in mission control *did* know how unpleasant things were. Yet somehow, "take the big metal rectangle, with sharp corners that can definitely puncture your spacesuit, all the way back to the shuttle, even though you can barely move your arms, and are so tired you're seeing black spots out of the corner of your eyes," was a reasonable ask.

Kris wasn't going to do what they wanted her to do with it. But she couldn't just abandon the panel where it was, free-floating in space. She had to secure it to the rest of the platform first; since the propulsion lattice on the underside couldn't go active until it was *correctly* aligned with the other six panels (the hookups were as misaligned as the holes) there actually *was* a risk that it would get knocked into an undesired vector.

As personally entertaining as Kris might find this, she happened to live in a place that would react poorly to being struck by a five-foot-by-ten-foot, nine-inch thick piece of metal. She couldn't risk it floating free and choosing violence.

———

SHE SECURED the panel in one spot, lining up two holes with one another and passing the screw through it. This left the edges off by a small but noticeable degree (up close; it looked fine from a distance) but ensured the panel wouldn't be going anywhere.

The next step was to retrieve the toolkit—a bulky square box with safety-rounded corners that attached to the belt around her waist—and disengage from the space platform.

She had an untethered spacewalk from there, back to the shuttle.

This would have been much easier if the shuttle was closer to the platform than it currently was. The *reason* it wasn't closer was the same reason the ESS itself was substantially further away, and that reason was massively stupid.

Essentially, they couldn't get so close to the space platform for someone viewing them from the surface to use the shuttle or ESS for scale. The company's bottom line depended on investors thinking it was larger than it was, and as a consequence of that, Kris's untethered spacewalk to the shuttle airlock was about four times longer than it *had* to be.

Kris hated the rule, for obvious reasons, but had yet to make a big stink about it, because she wasn't all that concerned about doing an untethered walk and so far, none of other crew members had objected. Yes, it was the *riskiest* part of a trip, but that honestly wasn't saying too much when just being *outside* came with massive inherent risk.

She disconnected from the platform, oriented herself on the shuttle, and gave her thrusters a small boost. The thrusters were attached to the suit itself, which added significant bulk to the outfit. (If they were on the surface, she probably wouldn't be able to stand.) She could fire them in any direction and, in doing so, travel in any direction. This was what made the untethered walks so risky; all she had to do was fire one off in the wrong direction for a little too long, and nobody would ever see her again.

"Looking good, Kris," Davina said. "Keep on that vector, and I'll see you in."

"That's affirmed," Kris said. Her eyes were on a free-floating tether on the left side of the shuttle, that was extended about twenty feet from the hull. She would be entering the shuttle through the airlock, but the risky part of this ended when she attached herself to that tether; they could pull her into the shuttle from there, if they had to.

"Ground says you're looking fine," Dav added. This had less to do with Kris's vector than it did with Kris's health. They were monitoring her vitals.

"Affirm," Kris said.

Kris's heartrate didn't go up during untethered spacewalks. To everyone at mission control, this made her some kind of unicorn. To Kris, it just meant she was either fully numb to the risk, or bored.

At about halfway to the shuttle's tether, something really peculiar happened, in an otherwise unremarkable region of space at the edge of Kris's vision.

"Hey, something weird," she said.

"What's wrong?" Davina asked.

Kris turned her head to the left, to get a better look, and gasped.

"Guys," she said, "I think I see…"

Then her radio shrieked, and whole universe went dark.

MORRIS

MORRIS ESTEBAN HAD ALREADY BEEN UP for seventeen hours when everything fell apart.

The Monterrey campus of Ellis Aerospace was one of those places business magazines took photos of, to show how great some people have it. The "some people" in this case was people who had agreed to work for Max Ellis in some capacity, in exchange for any approximation of a personal life and/or a soul.

Sure, they had it good. They worked in an office building with windows, and live plants, and free food, and a *jazz bar*, and oh yes, private bunk space if they, oh, who knows, felt like sleeping over, instead of going home to that apartment on the other side of the city, the one where the soon-to-be-estranged wife and kids live, with dying houseplants, fewer windows and no jazz bar whatsoever.

According to Ellis Aero, the reason they'd set up shop in Mexico was, 1: more land, for less, to build out the gloriously large and inviting campus they don't want anybody to leave, and 2: because the closer to the equator, the easier it was to launch objects into space. (This had to do with leveraging the Earth's rotational speed, and was why NASA hung out in Florida and Texas.)

These were good, decent reasons, but they weren't the *real* reasons. The real reasons were that they could build more cheaply in Mexico, ignore safety regulations with an alarming degree of impunity, and use tax pesos (Ellis Aero's space program was funded in part with public money) without having to disclose *how* they used it or what they found while using it.

Taken together, Ellis Aerospace held an advantage, when it came to launching people into space, with a timeline that made NASA look like they weren't doing anything at all. That they were absolutely not doing it safely didn't seem to matter to anybody, and probably wouldn't until Ellis Aerospace lost one of their astronauts.

(Even then, who knows? Max Ellis's spin machine was brilliant, and possibly unstoppable. Morris was pretty sure they'd find a way to turn it into a win.)

What it all added up to, was that the people on the ground—and Morris was in charge of a few of them—were in a perpetual state of exhaustion, keeping alive six off-planet people who were *also* in a perpetual state of exhaustion, while using equipment that was, at times, not up to the task.

They were well *paid*, which was nice, and they had a place on the facility to crash if they wanted to, which was also nice, and again, there was the free food and the jazz bar. But it would have been great if the high-tech future they all pretended to be living in wasn't just a shiny façade nailed onto a suboptimal infrastructure.

Sixteen of the seventeen hours for which Morris was awake had been spent in the main mission control room, an area that looked exactly like how one might expect it to look if someone said, "picture mission control." They had big screens on a wall. They had a raked floor with rows of computers. They had a glassed-off viewing area in the back of the room. They did *not* have a large staff filling the rows in front of the computers, and they only occasionally had anyone in the viewing area. This wasn't necessarily because the Monterrey team was doing less than the people in the Platonic ideal of mission control; mostly, it was just that modern computing power enabled one person to do what they used to need three for.

When they weren't launching something into space or retrieving something *from* space, the room was mostly empty; the day-to-day support work of Morris and his team happened in there, but didn't have to.

Today, they *were* in there, and the task was, primarily, to support the addition of the latest panel to the Ellis space platform. Morris was on duty during the initial launch of the shuttle from the hub, and he was supposed to remain there through the completion of the task, and the return of the shuttle to the hub again. That was the plan. When the panel didn't *fit*, he and the team went about figuring out why and asking the secondary support teams what to do about it, and then relaying that information back to Commander Standard and the rest of the team.

What Krista Standard decided to do with that information was out of his hands.

By the *end* of hour sixteen—with Kris adamantly refusing to follow the recommended course (not that he blamed her)—Mo decided he could use a nap, so he handed off his duties to Adrian Foley, the most senior person in the room after him, and took refuge in one of the bunk rooms down the hall.

Could he have gone home? Probably. Adrian was perfectly qualified to support the team on her own, and had only been on duty for eight hours. But Morris didn't have a wife or girlfriend to go home to, and home was forty minutes away, which was forty minutes of sleep he wouldn't be getting.

He may have dozed off a little, but when Adrian knocked on

the door—and then opened it, without waiting for a response—
he didn't feel particularly rested.

"Sorry," she said. "It's important. We just lost contact with
the entire ESS team."

———

EVERYONE IN MISSION control was in a state of organized
chaos, with people talking over each other and throwing seem-
ingly random computer outputs onto the big screen. The
problem in the moment was that they had no information to
work off of, beyond what Adrian told Morris when she first
showed up in his bunk room: every ESS feed had gone dead at
the same time.

This was impossible, which was why everyone was freaking
out in nerd, by arguing with numbers, outputs and screen
prompts.

Morris stepped into the middle of the room, raised his hand,
whistled loudly to shut everybody up, and said, "Tell me *exactly*
what happened."

They all tried to do that at the same time, which was no
good, so he whistled again. "If you can't do this calmly," he said,
"I'm gonna ask for raised hands. Adrian, you first."

"We don't know what happened," she said. "It's like a cord
was cut. One minute they were there, the next minute they
weren't."

"Okay, but there *is* no cord," Morris said. "We have,
what, ten or fifteen feeds? The main hub, the Habitat, the
shuttle, all six of their private channels, the direct to Susie,
the medical data feeds... what *exactly* do we *have*, and not
have?"

"This is what I'm saying," she said. "We lost *all* of that, at
the same time. Like everyone up there just stopped being up

THE WRONG SIDE OF SUNDOWN   23

there. It even affected the space platform; we're not getting well-ness bounce-backs anymore."

"Then it's us," Mo said. "We're one central area talking to many; it *has* to be us. Pedro?"

"I checked," I.T. guy Pedro said. "We're solid."

"I don't believe you," Mo said. "People, this is why we have a disaster recovery room; has anyone woken up Singapore?"

"Not yet," Adrian said.

"It'll take some time to spin them up," Pedro said, jumping on the nearest landline. "I'll make the call."

"Half an hour or less," Mo said. "That's what we were promised."

"I'll remind them."

The mission control disaster recovery room existed in the event something cataclysmic were to happen to the main location in Monterrey. It was one of the few system redundancies Ellis Aerospace spent real money on, possibly because everyone agreed that it would look bad if their astronauts died because someone nuked or otherwise disabled the main site.

They'd never executed the disaster recovery plan, outside of the monthly tests. In those tests, it took considerably less than a half an hour, but since they were conducted with plenty of advance warning, that wasn't really a useful metric.

"What were they doing before we lost them?" Mo asked.

"Kris was on a free walk to the shuttle," Adrian said.

"Untethered?"

"Yes."

"Sandee and Paul were both sleeping," Darius said, looking over a readout on his screen. Darius was the team's medical doctor. "Paul in the shuttle, Sandee in the Habitat. Davina was awake and waiting on Kris to return, also in the shuttle. Alan and Josip... I don't know what they were doing, but they were awake, and also in the Habitat. The only unusual event was a slight spike in Commander Standard's heartrate, just before we lost contact."

"A spike," Morris repeated. "In *Kris's* heartrate."

"That's what the instruments say."

Kris had the steady heartbeat of a sociopath so, that was pretty odd. "Anybody else on the team record a spike?"

"Just her," Darius said.

"All right, let's file that away for now. What do we have for audio?"

"We... probably should have started there," Adrian said. She nodded to Jorge, who ran comms. "Play it."

Jorge nodded. "This is the last thing we got from them," he said. He hit play, and then the room heard Kris's voice: "Guys, I think I see..."

Then there was a burst of static that lasted about two seconds, and that was all.

"Play it again," Mo said.

Jorge did, and then again, and again, before Morris was satisfied that they weren't going to get anything else out of it. If the recording had been made anywhere other than *space*, he might now be asking Jorge to mine the audio for some kind of background noise. But there wasn't going to be any.

"What do we think she saw?" Mo asked.

The entire room shrugged collectively.

"We don't know," Adrian said. "But that's why we don't think the problem is down here."

Morris sat down in one of the many extra chairs, and asked Jorge to play it a couple more times.

"We're talking about a complete communications blackout," Mo said, after a minute of thought. "Solar flare?"

"Already checked," Adrian said. "If there was one, it went unobserved."

"Something big enough to do this to the ESS team would

have had a measurable effect on planetary communications at the same time," Jorge said. "We didn't see that."

"Did you check nearby communications satellites?" Mo asked.

"Not directly," Jorge said. "But if there had been a localized telecom blackout, we'd have heard."

"Okay, a cosmic burst, then," Morris offered. "Some rogue cosmic ray that fried their electronics."

"The distance from the platform to the ESS was about a quarter of a mile at the time of the incident," Adrian said. "If there's a type of cosmic ray that's *that* energetic and *that* wide, we've never seen one before."

"All right, but not impossible," Morris said. "We'll have to come back to that. What else?"

"An EMP could do it," Pedro said. It looked like he was on hold with Singapore, which annoyed Morris enormously. They should have been ready for a call. "It'd have to be set off nearby, but something like that could take out the whole Ellis mission scope without necessarily reaching any of the satellites."

"An *attack*," Mo said. "That's what you're saying."

"Someone would have to fire it from the planet," Adrian said. "Using a rocket that could reach their orbital level. It would have to be something nobody on the Sunset Station team saw until the last minute, and that we never detected. But it's not impossible."

"Not impossible is the best we can hope for right now," Morris said. "Who do we have in the U.S. military that we can call? A rocket fired into space would have set off a lot of alarm bells."

"Sure," Jorge said. "Except how many countries have a missile that could do that? Pentagon's the prime suspect here, Mo."

"Hold it, hold it, hold it," Darius said. "The station wasn't *over* the U.S. when this happened."

"He's right," Pedro said.

"*China* was," Jorge said. "So was Russia."

"What if they were nuked?" Pedro asked. "Not an EMP, just a straight-up nuclear bomb. China and Russia both have nukes, too."

"Why would they do that?" Darius asked. "Why would *anyone* do that?"

"Why would anyone attack them at *all*?" Pedro said. "No reason, right? Except someone did."

"Hang on, hang on," Morris said. "Everybody, take a step back. First off, I'm not the rocket scientist in the room, but I don't think conventional nuclear weapons are built to reach upper orbit. Second, if a nuclear *bomb* went off in the night sky over east Asia, we'd have heard about it already. Confirm, but I'm pretty sure we're not talking about a nuke."

"But it *was* an attack," Jorge said.

"We don't know that yet either, Jorge," Morris said. "We have to rule out the obvious explanations first, guys. If it isn't any of them, that leaves the crazy explanations."

Adrian looked at him, bemused. "Do you have crazy explanation in mind, Mo?"

"One or two. And no, I'm not going to tell you what they are." He checked his watch. "I've gotta go tell Max Ellis we may have just lost Sunset Station. Let me know the minute Singapore is live."

ALAN

ALAN WAS in the middle of a game of backgammon when the lights went out.

Living on a space station meant accepting that the list of things that could possibly go wrong on a given day—and, in going wrong, could cause the deaths of everybody involved—was much longer than if he was *not* living on a space station.

For example, a broken window in *space* was a much bigger deal. So was an abrupt lack of food or water. It was also (aside from life aboard a submersible) the only place where running out of breathable air was a valid concern.

Then there was the list of things Alan never expected to have to worry about, while aboard a space station, but which could easily happen on Earth. A power failure, for instance. Sure, on Earth, this was definitely a problem but, like "tornadoes," and "getting struck by lightning," it didn't make sense to worry about it in space.

This was not to say that a total loss of power on the ESS was *unfathomable*; it was just so highly unlikely that, were it to happen, an extraordinary explanation would be required. This was because the station was powered by a large bank of rechargeable batteries, any one of which could keep the lights on, and the heat, and the oxygen, and so on, for weeks. The batteries were recharged by the sun. Unlike food, water, and oxygen, sunlight—in space—was an inexhaustible resource.

This was why, when they lost power, at first Alan simply didn't know what to do.

The game of backgammon was between himself and Josip. (According to the tally, this was their 592nd game since the beginning of their bucket vacation. Josip was leading, 301-291 which—Alan had to point out every few minutes—was effectively a tie. Josip did not agree.) They were in the middle of the common area, at the table set up specifically for board games, while Sandee was behind a curtain in her private bunk on the other side of the room, either sleeping or engaging with the internet. Or both; her multitasking abilities were fearsome.

They had the radio tuned to the mission the others were in the middle of. Consequently, they heard Kris's last words, and the burst of static.

That was when the lights went out.

Alan and Josip sat motionless for several seconds, before speaking.

"Well, this is peculiar," Alan said.

"Shh," Josip said. "Listen. Don't move, and listen."

"Guys?" Sandee shouted from her bunk. "Did I go blind, or…"

"Don't move, little sister," Josip barked.

"Um, okay," she said. "Not moving."

Josip called Sandee "little sister" as a term of endearment nobody else even attempted. He was the oldest member of the crew, and she was the youngest, and that was probably what it came out of. It could also have been a reaction to how she referred to Josip and Alan, i.e., "my two dads." Josip seemed to prefer a brother-sister dynamic.

"What are you thinking, Josip?" Alan asked.

"I am thinking that we are on the end of a chamber that is rapidly spinning around a space station that has just lost all power. Can you hear?"

The darkness wasn't *total*, only nearly so. (The bucket had no windows. Someone figured out pretty early on that putting a window in something that was spinning as fast as it had to spin in order to achieve 1G was a bad idea.) The room had luminescent strips on the edges of all the corners and along the floor, something he had not known about before. Now that his eyes were adjusting, he could make out Josip, as a void in the luminescence.

"I can almost *see* you now," Alan said. "But I don't hear anything."

"Exactly," Josip said. "You *should* hear something."

"The air is out," Sandee said.

"Yes, but that is not our biggest concern," Josip said.

"Heat's out too," Sandee added. "Think we'll suffocate or freeze to death first?"

"Oh," Alan said. "The stabilizers. *That's* what I'm not hearing."

"Power's gonna come *back*, right?" Sandee asked. They could hear her rustling around in the living area.

"Don't move!" both of them shouted.

"Okay, okay," she said. "Why not?"

"Because when we lost the light, the air and the heat, we also lost the centrifugal stabilizers," Alan said.

"Oh," she said. Then she thought about it some more and added, "Ohhh. Well that's terrific. What do we do?"

THE PROBLEM WAS THIS: the bucket was spinning around an axis—the main hub—offset on the other side by a metal cube with the same approximate mass as the bucket. There was an engine in the hub whose only job was to get the bucket spinning up to the right speed to match sea level Earth gravity, and then to make sure it stayed there.

There was no resistance—no friction—in space, to slow down the spin. However, the connection point between the hub and the cables, connecting both the bucket and the counter-mass (it was a track attached to a brace) *did* have friction, which *could* slow it down. In short, the bucket couldn't spin forever, without getting goosed up to speed periodically.

That wasn't the issue, and actually, slowing down wouldn't be a problem at all; it would be a solution. The *problem* was that the same mechanism that kept the bucket going at the appropriate spin also had stabilizers built in to offset incidental angular movement.

Any sideways motion—that is, a motion in a direction other than the axis—created vibrations that would magnify with each rotation. It might take ten thousand spins, but eventually, without some kind of stabilizing mechanism in place to dampen the effect, it would tear the station apart. And ten thousand spins wasn't a whole lot.

None of this would be a problem if the ESS had a permanent, fixed wheel that spun around the main hub. It didn't, because the retractable bucket was easier to get into space—the entire station was sent up in one large rocket—and much cheaper. The Ellis Space Station was a prime example of innovative physics paired with a lowest-bidder mentality. Thanks to that, all three of them were probably about to die.

"WE SHOULD ASSUME there was a short in the main hub," Josip said. "As this is the most plausible explanation."

Alan could think of a bunch of other potential explanations that he thought were probably just as good, but this was in Josip's wheelhouse; he probably knew better.

"The system has an auto restart function," Josip continued, "which should have, by now, initiated. It hasn't, and now the reset must be executed manually."

"We can't do that from here," Sandee said. "Has to be done from the hub."

"Are you sure?" Alan asked.

"Positive," she said. "Main systems aren't routed to us. All we have is comms, and that's out too. And I don't want to keep harping on this, but we're probably going to run out of oxygen soon?"

"We will likely succumb to CO_2 poisoning before then," Josip said. "The scrubbers are also off."

"Well that's *terrific*, dad, thanks," she said.

Sandee's primary expertise was in computer tech; she understood more than any of them about the base code that ran the ESS. Josip, decidedly more old-school, knew how to run (and repair) a space station as if there was no computer. Both of their skillsets were more relevant to the situation than Alan's; he was the first out the door in a spacewalk, and the most competent pilot—he came from the Air Force—and he was also, technically, *in charge* of this particular pod, although that also didn't seem terribly relevant at the moment.

"So we need to get to bridge of the hub, somehow," Alan said, "preferably before we run out of air, freeze to death, or succumb to toxic levels of CO_2. How do we do that?"

"We have to stop the rotation," Josip said.

"We can't stop the rotation without power," Sandee pointed

out. "And we can't get the power back unless we stop the rotation."

"And we can't move," Alan said.

"Who the fuck designed this stupid station?" Sandee asked.

"We *can* stop the rotation," Josip said. Josip's head, silhouetted by luminescent tape on the wall behind him, tilted upward. "There's a manual brake at the hinge point."

Alan followed Josip's gaze, to the glowing ladder rungs that extended up the side of the tunnel leading to the hub.

"Uhhh, okay," Alan said. "Yeah. That seems like a really bad idea."

▭

THE BUCKET WAS CONNECTED to the hub by a string of load-bearing cables threaded through a collapsible tunnel. The cables were basically a giant Slinky; when the bucket was spun out, the cables were almost straight, and the tunnel was narrow. The ladder, which extended along with the tunnel, was anchored at the gasket at the hub end and to the roof of the bucket at the other, and ran flush with one side.

When they wanted to stop the spin—which, again, was ordinarily executed by someone in the main hub, and which required electricity—they applied brakes at the contact point, while at the same time, tiny reverse thrusters were fired from the underside of the bucket and of the counter-mass (which was also attached to the axis via Slinky cables, albeit shorter ones with no tunnel) and the controlled slowdown began.

As the bucket's spin slowed, the Slinky and the tunnel inside of it accordioned—rotating the bucket counterclockwise, albeit gently—and the ladder collapsed. On the final revolution, the top of the tunnel would come into alignment with an airlock hatch that led to the main hub, and stop.

With no simulated gravity to contend with, the occupants of the bucket at that point would be free to float through the short tunnel and into the space station.

When operated by a computer program that was designed to adjust for unexpected force changes, it was a nice, smooth process that almost made one forget what a massively stupid solution it was to an unnecessary problem. (If the space station had a fixed wheel that extended, say, twice as far as the bucket's, not only would they not have to *stop* it from spinning to get off, they could probably have windows.)

Nobody had ever tried applying the brakes manually, without the correcting thrusters. Nobody had ever gone into the tunnel while the bucket was in full spin (although the existence of the ladder implied it was considered feasible by someone on the design team.) Nobody had ever been *in* the tunnel as it was collapsing, while holding onto a ladder that was *also* collapsing. And nobody had ever tested the manual brake to see if it actually worked.

Hypothetically, all of those, "it has never been done before" things had been tested by someone before the ESS even left Earth. But this was Ellis Aerospace. Yes, it was possible the braking had been tested. It was also possible that someone put the brake and the ladder there because it seemed like a good idea, and nobody vetted it after that.

Most exigencies had some kind of procedural buildout, but since it was Alan's job to know all such procedures—and since he didn't have one for this scenario—he was pretty sure they were about to be the first to test the scenario.

"If I have this right," Sandee was saying, as the three of them eyed the distance between the floor and the ceiling. She was shining a hand light she'd brought from her bunk, which only helped a little. "Someone's gotta go up the tunnel of death, and brake us hard enough to slow the spin, but not so hard that the inertia snaps the tunnel in half and sends us off into wherever."

"Yes, little sister, that's correct," Josip said.

"That's *entirely* insane, Jo."

"You are not wrong."

Sandee had just joined them in the main room. This took about ten minutes of the slowest walking she could manage without falling over. The three of them agreed it would be better if most of the movement took place on the same axis as the connecting tunnel, going forward, and also, that they would need her help getting Josip up there once she made it into the middle of the room.

"So, *exactly* what do I do when I get to the top?" she asked.

"No, no, no," Josip said.

"*Josip's* going," Alan said.

"*I* am going," Jo said, at the same time.

"I'm lighter than you are," she said to Josip. "And shorter than you," she said to Alan. "And I'm more *flexible* than both of you."

"Absolutely not," Josip said. "I will not allow it."

It was difficult to tell if Josip's objection was driven by an instinctive protectiveness toward his erstwhile younger-sister/daughter, a concern that she would be unable to do it, or a need to not risk someone else's life for something that was his idea.

"What do you mean, *allow?*" she asked, and now she was pissed. ("Never piss off Sandee," was a fundamental tenet of their pod.)

"Hold it," Alan said, looking up again. He was trying to gauge the distance to the ladder's bottom rung, in the dark. It was not an inconsequential gap; that much he knew. What the bucket lacked in floor space it made up for with a high ceiling.

It made no sense at all to have a ladder that didn't reach the floor, but since it also didn't make sense to have them maneuvering around a ladder in the middle of the room all the time, he guessed that there was a mechanism to lower it, that they didn't have access to, because nobody planned for a total power failure.

They were going to have to either lift or *launch* someone at the ladder, was the point; it made more sense to try that with Sandee—who Alan thought he could probably *throw* if he had to—than Josip, who he doubted he could even pick up.

"She's right, Jo," he said. "It makes more sense to send her."

"Alan, I absolutely..."

"Decision's final," Alan said. "Now let's figure out how to get her up there."

IF THEIR LIFE didn't depend on getting this done, it probably would have been funny. Three people, all with advanced degrees in theoretical and applied physics, aeronautics, and engineering (plus a lot of less applicable experiences, like computer science, and poli sci,) couldn't figure out how to get one of them to a ladder roughly eighteen feet above their heads.

Stacking furniture got them close—or, it *seemed* like they were close, in the dark—but not close enough. Putting Sandee on Alan shoulders, and then Alan on Josip's shoulders, didn't work either, even when they had Josip stand on the table first. They considered getting a sheet, putting Sandee in the sheet, and having Alan and Josip launch her straight up, but the risk—that she might miss the ladder, come back down and break an arm, or her neck—was too great.

But the *sheet* was the right idea. They just had to use it differently.

After collecting all the bedsheets—which they didn't bother

to do *slowly*, because all the movement that had come out of trying to get her up there via more conventional means had undoubtedly already doomed them to a fatal torqueing cascade in the near future—they tied the sheets together, end-to-end. Then they tied one end to a two pound hand weight, and took turns tossing the weight up in the air, the goal being to get it through one of the rungs.

It took seventy-two tries. (Alan had the winning toss.) By then, the bucket had developed a noticeable wobble.

"Remember what you have to do?" Josip asked, as he helped Sandee up onto the table, from which she would be rope-climbing the rest of the way to the ladder.

"I find the handbrake on the rim," she said, "pull it forward to extend the handle, and then pull *back* on it, hard."

"But not *too* hard," Alan said.

"The Goldilocks of not too hard," she said. "I know. That'll engage the brake. Then I just hold on until we're safe. Or, you know. Very much not safe."

The bucket shimmied then; they all felt it.

"That is bad," Josip said.

"Yep," Sandee said. "Counterbalance me, huh?"

She gave a tug on the blanket. Alan, holding the end tied to the hand weight, braced himself. Josip, standing next to him, grabbed another spot. With the sheet taut, Sandee began to climb.

PAUL

PAUL WOKE up in the dark.

Sleeping in space—when not on the bucket—meant being stuck in a sleeping bag that was tied down. It didn't *feel* all that much, to the sleeper, like *they* were the ones being tied down—there was room between the body and the bag, that allowed some freedom of motion. That wasn't a problem. But the perpetual sense of weightlessness, while easy to rationalize when awake, was really hard on the unconscious mind. This was why, nearly every sleep cycle, Paul had dreams of falling, that is when he wasn't having nightmares about being stuffed into a chimney, or tied to a roof rack, or about to be fired out of a cannon.

It was perhaps because of the dreams that none of them slept much or slept well any longer. It could also be because they were in a setting with no day and night while using brains programmed for a diurnal existence, or it could just be the perpetual stress that came from living in small, habitable pockets, surrounded on all sides by the most lethal environment imaginable. Whatever the reason, none of the crew got more than three or four hours of sleep at a time—even when they tried —unless they were in the bucket.

(This had been going on for long enough that scholarly papers had been written about the crew. Those papers warned about gradual cognitive deterioration leading to permanent brain damage, which was why nobody at Sunset Station—other than Paul—had read any of the papers.)

Rather than solve for the lack of sleep, the medical advisory team instituted mandatory nap schedules. It was for this reason that Paul happened to be in the middle of a nap while also in the middle of a shuttle mission. His task, once Kris finished and returned to the shuttle for her own nap, would be to go out and hook up the electronics on the underside of the panel.

Waking up in darkness and silence wasn't a part of the schedule.

It wasn't actually *total* darkness; the shuttle had its share of windows, including a big dome cockpit that gave them a 140 degree view, and exposed the interior—depending on what direction they were facing—to direct (filtered) sunlight, reflected sunlight, or starlight. They were angled away from the sun at the moment, so there wasn't *much* light, but there was enough that Paul knew his eyes were open, that he hadn't gone blind, and that something was wrong.

"Guys?" he shouted, wiggling to the top of the bag. "What's going on? Did I oversleep?"

From the perspective of the sleep cot—it was attached to the ceiling in the back corner of the shuttle's main chamber—it didn't look like there was anyone in the cockpit seat. This was somehow more disturbing than the lack of power; Dav and Kris wouldn't *both* go outside without waking him first.

How long have *I been out?* he wondered. He put his hand up to his face, half-expecting to discover a long beard, indicating it had been *weeks,* and he was in the middle of some weird-as-hell science fiction story. But his chin was no more stubbly than it had been before the nap.

He freed himself fully from the bag and maneuvered around until his boots were in contact with the floor and the magnets engaged. Then, and only then, did he realize he was *not* alone; Davina was there too, floating in a corner of the main chamber.

"Dav?" he called out. "Davina, are you okay?"

He grabbed her ankle and pulled her down to the floor. She still had on the headset that went with the command console; she must have been in the cockpit when whatever happened to the power happened.

He checked her vitals. They were strong; she wasn't dead, just unconscious.

"Davina, wake up," he said. "Something's happened."

He was debating an adrenaline shot or a slap across the face, when her eyes fluttered open.

"Paul?" she said. "What are you doing?"

"Something's wrong," he said. "I think we've lost power. Where's Kris?"

"Kris... Kris!" she gasped. Davina scrambled to a vertical position, using Paul as an anchor, and launched herself at the dome window.

"Where is she?" she asked, bouncing from one viewing angle to the next. "I don't see her. Paul... she was right there. We both, we have to..."

"Calm down, Dav," he said, catching up to her. He took her by the hands, in part because with all her flailing he was worried she was going to damage something, and because she looked about ready to start hitting herself in the head or rend clothing.

With the others, it was an open secret that Kris and Davina were in a relationship. With *Paul* it wasn't a secret anything; he'd been there for every step of that relationship, and in some weird way just short of a throuple, he was a part of it. (He was more like the gay best friend, or the gay third wheel, or the gay cousin or, well, pick a relationship type: as long as it was prefaced with "gay" it would be close enough.)

"Tell me what happened," he said. "Just walk me through it."

"We have to find her, Paul," she said. "She needs us."

"We can't help her until we help ourselves," he said. "We're dead in space, and I don't know how long we've been like this. We may be about to run out of air."

She took a few deep breaths (as if testing the air,) and started to come back to herself a little. If this were a normal(er) time, he'd be checking her for a concussion. That would have to wait.

"There's spare oxygen tanks," she said. "Um. Under the deck. And there are the tanks attached to the suits. But we'll *need* those, to go out and... can we even get to the airlock without power?"

"I think so," he said. The airlock door was opened with a wheel not dissimilar to a bank lock dial, or submarine hatch. There was a hydraulic component that made it easier to open and close, but as long as the outer door wasn't open, he should be able to manage it without. "Do you remember what happened?"

"There was a, a surge. The whole board lit up... that's all I remember."

Paul bent down over the control panel, and sniffed. Electrical engineering wasn't his specialty, but he knew what smoke smelled like. "I don't think it shorted," he said. "I'd smell it, right?"

"That doesn't mean it didn't short out," she said. She ducked down under the console to have a look. "You can't expect electricals to work out here the way they would on Earth; a spark from a short and we're probably all dead."

She slid back out from under the panel.

"There are dampeners," she said, "and breakers to handle an overload. They would have kicked in way before too much energy hit the wiring and caused an overheat like you're thinking. Which is good."

"Why's that good?" he asked.

"It means, the problem isn't that we don't have power. The problem is, we're cut *off* from our power source. We just have to find the breakers."

"You don't know where they are?"

"I know where they're supposed to be, but who knows if they're there? This is Ellis we're talking about." She sat up and looked at the airlock door in the back of the chamber. "I hope you're right about opening that, because I'm going to need a light source and a toolkit, and those are both on the other side of the door."

MAX

MAX ELLIS'S day began the same as it always did, with a protein shake and a jog along the fence of his private sanctuary that wasn't actually a sanctuary. It was *actually* a private, fifty-acre estate, protected by electrified fences and AI-operated aerial drones, with state-of-the-art facial recognition software that matched hits against fifteen databases, two of which were only supposed to be used by the US government, and five of which were, strictly speaking, completely illegal due to unsanctioned data collection. There were also dogs, and a ten person full-time human staff. But the people in Ellis Public Relations said "sanctuary" tested better than "estate," so it was a sanctuary.

After the jog came a quick shower and shave, and then he slipped into his branded outfit—black slacks, button-down white shirt, custom made blue hoodie, slip-on shoes—put on one of three Ellis Eyenet headsets, and joined his first meeting of the day.

Like the need for multiple headsets—he had three, because one couldn't hold a charge for a full day of constant use yet, which was definitely something the people at Ellis Wearables had to get their shit together on, and soon—and the "same outfit every day" approach to his clothing choices, Max wanted his days to go as seamlessly as they *could* go, with as few inconsequential decisions gumming up the works as possible. That way, he could focus on only what *was* consequential, or otherwise disruptive.

He took in an average of ninety-two meetings per day. These meetings happened all around the world, at all hours. The average meeting lasted forty-three minutes, and there remained only one thousand, four hundred and forty minutes in a day, so of course Max wasn't available for all of any one meeting.

Thus, across the entirety of the Ellis corporate empire, it was understood that every top-level meeting had to *include* Max Ellis, but Max Ellis would only be *available* for five to seven minutes of that meeting. Therefore, it was the responsibility of every team lead to present exactly and only what Max needed to hear that day, in one, tidy, five-to-seven minute window.

From the outside looking in, this probably sounded insane, but to Max's way of thinking, any manager unable to boil down whatever problem or issue they needed to escalate upward into a five-to-seven minute presentment didn't actually understand their job well enough to execute at a high level, and needed to be replaced.

(Many satellite offices attacked this mandate with real repressed-theater-geek creativity. There was one team in the superconductor group in Ohio that performed a six minute musical once a month. He always enjoyed their meetings, and made sure they knew it.)

On this day, Max's first meeting—which he took from the backseat of his luxury Ellis Auto—began at exactly 7:02 AM PST. It was with the heads of the ion battery factory in Rajasthan, and it was very boring. His time commitment lasted until 7:07, but by 7:05:30, he had pretty much stopped paying attention.

The second meeting, with the IP team in the UK, wouldn't require him until 7:15. This gave Max time to sift through the news, while Pete Stanton took the car out through the gates.

"How's your morning going?" Pete asked. He knew, thanks to a readout on the dash, that Max was between meetings, or he wouldn't have spoken.

"Just lovely, Pete. How's Janet?"

"She's doing great, sir. I'll tell her you asked."

Max wasn't supposed to have a driver. Ellis Auto's topline self-driving cars were supposed to eliminate the *need* for a driver, a point Max made publicly many, many times. And yet, there was Pete, behind the wheel.

The windows were all tinted, so there weren't many photos showing Max in a car with Pete driving, but it happened, and when it did—when someone called Max out on this—he got out of it by claiming Pete was in the car because he happened to be one of Max's personal assistants—which was true—but that he wasn't actually *driving* the car. Which was *not* true.

"We're only following the current regulations imposed by the State of California on self-driving vehicles," Max would explain. "I prefer to sit in the back, but since the regulations say we have to have someone in the driver's seat in the event 'something happens,'" (he would make dramatic air quotes here,) "Pete sits up at the wheel. But of course, he's not *driving*."

Sure, it was a lie, technically, but Max didn't think that was a fair take. The car really *could* drive itself, and Pete Stanton really *didn't* have to drive it; that was all true. It just wasn't the *full* truth.

The *full* truth, was that Ellis Auto's topline self-driving car technology team was about a decade away from rolling out an *actual* self-driving car. What would happen, if Pete put the car in self-drive mode, was that it would actually be piloted by a team of four-to-six people at a computer console in Suzhou.

All appearances aside, at the end of the day Max would rather Pete drive him around than a small team of sub-minimum wagers in mainland China.

They were heading to the California headquarters of Ellis Imagine, which was sort of a venture capital thinktank, and one of the places Max kept an office fulltime. He didn't *need* to go into the office, either on this day, or ever. But Max didn't like being alone for long periods. Considering he hardly ever dated, had no non-dating-specific social life to fall back on, and had made a *lot* of money on technology that was practically designed for the benefit of the self-isolated, this was a little ironic.

The 7:15 meeting went fine—no new lawsuits—and the 7:25 with the German auto parts division was so unmemorable he didn't make it to five minutes before bailing.

Things started to go wrong during the 7:39 meeting. The call was with another manufacturing team in a facility outside of Chicago—one of the smartglass groups—and things were fine there; they weren't the problem. Ellis Aero was the problem.

"Mr. Ellis," Pete Stanton said, over Max's audio feed. He would never do that unless it was serious; ergo, it was serious.

"Just a second, guys," Max said to the Chicago team. He muted them, turned the glasses transparent, and said, "What is it, Pete?"

"We have Monterrey breaking in, sir."

"Priority?"

"They said five."

"Shit, okay," Max said. He got back on with Chicago. "Ronnie, I just got a priority five, I've gotta drop," he said.

"A *five?*" Ronnie said. "Hope it's not too bad."

Every manager throughout the Ellis empire had learned to

embrace the threat priority matrix, which was yet another thing invented to keep people from bringing too many things to Max Ellis all at once. Priority one meant, get it to him by the end of the week. Priority two, by the end of the day, and three, within the hour. Priority four meant, get Max *right now*, because someone was getting sued, someone had died, or something was about to explode.

A priority five meant the world was ending.

Hardly anyone invoked five.

Max jumped off the Chicago call, and skimmed for the connection to Monterrey. In a few seconds, he was looking at a boardroom just off the mission control floor. Morris Esteban was there, alone, looking more exhausted than usual.

"I'm here, Mo," Max said. "Are they all dead?"

"Well?" he said. "We're not sure."

"Jesus Christ, I was kidding."

"I'm not. We lost contact with Sunset Station, on all feeds, at the same time."

Max knew a decent bit about the technology governing their communications with Sunset Station, so he understood that this was a fundamentally ridiculous statement. But Morris Esteban was no idiot. Max didn't *hire* idiots.

"I'm going to say that's not possible, Mo," Max said. "And then you're going to tell me it actually is, and I'm missing something."

"You're right, it shouldn't be possible," Morris said. "It's like someone took a pair of scissors to every tethered connection between them and the relay satellites. And before you ask, we checked all the relay satellites and they pinged us back. They're fine. We're thinking this may have been an attack."

"An EMP."

"Maybe."

"That would do it."

"Sure, but it doesn't really fit the evidence," Morris said. "Only, nothing else does either. Same with a nuclear bomb; it'd *work*, but we don't know how a bomb gets out there, and we don't have any other evidence for it."

"Some new kind of weapon," Max suggested.

"Again, sure, maybe. But we still have the same problem: how did it get there?"

"So, they might be dead. You're thinking they might be dead."

"I don't know *what* to think," Morris said. "For all we know, they're just fine, and wondering why we don't answer."

"Do you think that's possible?" Max asked.

"Honestly, no. But it's not *im*possible, and I'll take anything at this point."

"All right, what do you need?"

"Need?" Morris repeated. He sounded like it hadn't occurred to him to ask Max for help. "I just thought you'd want to hear about it as soon as possible. We're trying to get Singapore up to validate that this isn't a problem with the ground, but—"

"But what if it *was* an attack?" Max asked. "The sooner we can confirm that, the better."

"That's the thinking."

"We'll need to know if anyone detected a launch," Max said, not really talking to Morris so much as thinking out loud. "And we need eyes on Sunset Station. Not from the ground... we'd have to task a satellite."

"I don't have a satellite that can do that, in-house," Morris said.

"That's okay, I know someone who does. Hang tight, Mo; I'm coming to you." Max hung up before Morris could respond. "Pete, turn us around; we're going to the airport. Tell Verna I want to be in the air in an hour."

Pete, who had been working for Max long enough not to

question, immediately committed to a U-turn the team in Suzhou could never have pulled off remotely.

"We going to Mexico?" Pete asked.

"Yes, we are."

Max autodialed Anna, another of his personal assistants (he had seven.)

"Anna, I need you to cancel all my remaining meetings today. Nothing higher than a 4 comes to me."

"Yes, Mr. Ellis," she said. "Can I say why?"

"You cannot. Also, I need to speak to Marty Burgess. Get him for me."

"Marty...?"

"General Martin Burgess. He should be at the Pentagon. Have Tom pull up the military contracts for the number."

SANDEE

SANDEE'S CLIMB to the axis got easier the closer she was to the top, because she got lighter as she went. By the time she'd reached the brake, she was nearly weightless.

Once there, she had to feel around in the dark for the brake arm, which was up against the hard shell of the door at the top of the tunnel.

When the bucket wasn't spinning, the door lined up with an opening on the inside of the main hub, to allow free passage. That it had a brake on the outer rim was news to her, but knowing the technical specs of the station was Josip's sweet spot, not hers. *Her* job was computers, and social media engagement, two responsibilities that probably made no sense outside of the Ellis sphere.

(If they didn't make it out of this alive, the first time anyone on Earth would probably know about it would be when Sandee failed to show for one of her live engagements, or stop posting new media. To Josip and Alan, this was a sad commentary on their current reality; for her, it was just the way the world worked. No point in getting revved up about it.)

Once she unlocked the brake arm, she gave the arm one

tentative tug, to see how sensitive it was. This did hardly anything, so she tried a more robust tug, and that was nearly cataclysmic.

There was the hideous shriek of rubber-on-steel, along with an unpleasant burning smell that was bad anywhere, but especially in space. Then the bucket swung violently in the direction of the spin.

She felt it in the swaying of the ladder beneath her feet. Alan and Josip had it much worse; it sounded like a bowling alley had broken out in the bucket, when all the furniture (which should have been secured but which was not) plus the surprised, shouting occupants, were suddenly thrown toward one of the walls.

"Too fast!" Alan shouted, from below.

"Sorry!" Sandee said, coming off the brake. "You guys wanna brace yourselves before I try this again?"

"Now that we know which direction in which we are spinning," Jo said, "we can try."

Her third attempt landed at a midpoint between the two extremes. The system still shrieked, but not as much, Josip and Alan braced themselves appropriately, and the furniture (based on the silence) remained where it was.

There was also no drastic, explosive decompression as a consequence of the bucket breaking off the connecting tunnel and launching into deep space and killing them, which was great.

All that was terrific, but if this was the hardest she could apply the brakes, it was going to take an *awfully* long time for them to stop.

The normal spin-down time was four hours, with the hydraulic air brake and the external boosters both going. The experience, from inside, was akin to gradually being introduced to a weightless environment, while otherwise not moving. (The only time they ever felt the sideways pull was at the beginning of the spin, or the end of it.) It could definitely slow down faster, if the situation called for them to do that; it would make for a worse experience, but it could be done. It could also, technically, stop almost immediately, but that was a setting reserved for when there was nobody in the bucket. If someone *was* inside for that, they'd be turned into a lumpy paste.

She needed it to take less than four hours, because any one of the four potential deaths facing them—lack of oxygen, a surplus of carbon dioxide, a lack of heat, or a lethal sideways torque—could take them out in less than that amount of time, and probably would. Plus, she was pretty positive she couldn't hold the brake for that long, even under ideal conditions, and these were very much not ideal conditions. She couldn't see anything—she'd left the light with Alan—which in and of itself wasn't a problem, but she was also inside a giant Slinky, standing on a collapsing ladder. She could hear and feel it moving, but not *see* it.

After what felt like an hour—it probably was less than that—she tried tying the brake in place.

The pants for her Ellis-Aero-issued leisure time outfit came with a drawstring, rather than a proper belt. (The standard crew jumpsuit didn't have a real belt either; belts weren't that important in zero gravity.) It wasn't nearly strong enough to do the job; she didn't even try. Instead, she slipped out of the long sleeved shirt, (she had to release the brake to do this,) rolled it up, attached one end to the brake arm, and the other to one of the steel supports. The shirt was up to the task—the tensile strength of an astronaut's uniform shirt being pretty impressive—but there was no way to get a knot to hold, on either end. After about ten minutes of stumbling about at it, she gave up and went back to holding the brake in place the hard way.

After another few minutes of holding it there, she realized she was getting lightheaded.

Sandee wasn't the person to go to for advanced calculations on the properties of gas, but she knew carbon dioxide was heavier than oxygen, so if anyone was having a time with CO_2 it would be Alan and Jo, before her. If it *was* carbon dioxide making her light-headed, the others were probably already dead. She didn't like that possibility at all, and went looking for another one.

"The air is thinner up here," she declared. That could be it, given she was on the wrong end of a giant centrifuge.

Could also just be exhaustion; she'd been halfway through her sleep cycle when the power went out, and she couldn't remember the last time she ate.

Or, again, the others were already dead and she was next.

"Guys, how's it going down there?" she asked.

After a super-long silence, Alan answered.

"We're okay," he said. "I'm okay."

"Josip?"

No answer.

"Jo?" she repeated.

"Don't worry about him," Alan said. "Keep going."

"Uh," she said. She was now *very* worried about Josip. "I was gonna ask, if the gravity's down enough, maybe one of you can make it up here? I could use a break."

"I don't think I can reach you yet," Alan said.

"Okay," she said. "All right, here's what I'm gonna do. Figure... I figure this fuckin' accordion I'm stuck in... the more compressed it gets, the more stress it can take, yeah?"

"That follows. But I don't know how much it's—"

"I know, but it should hold better than when we first tried the brake. I'm saying, I'm gonna slow us down faster. I can't pull on this brake forever and you guys are almost out of air, so. If we go, we go."

After a decent pause, Alan said, "we'll brace ourselves."

"You do that."

Sandee repositioned herself in the tunnel to get better leverage. The harder she pulled, the greater it resisted being pulled; she was going to need both arms. That meant sticking one leg off the ladder and against one of the tunnel's support cables. She'd be all right as long as it didn't move *too* much during the spindown.

"Here goes," she muttered. Then she pulled, hard.

As before, the brakes shrieked, and the bucket shifted in the direction of the spin, but this time she didn't relent; instead, she pulled even harder.

It did not fall apart. They did not die. And the spin slowed at an observable rate. She felt the tunnel collapsing near her brace foot, and the ladder beneath her other foot shift.

Something she couldn't have anticipated: the rung she had her boot on was part of a different ladder section than the rung above it. She didn't realize this until the two sections had already begun to collapse.

Her foot was caught before she could do anything about it.

Well, she thought, once she concluded wiggling free wasn't an option, *this is gonna suck.*

She pulled harder on the brake.

MAX

GENERAL MARTIN BURGESS was the kind of useful ass every large organization needed. He was stubborn, performatively offended by price quotes—as if the money was coming out of his own pocket—didn't understand how most of the technology he was responsible for obtaining worked, and worse, didn't know his understanding was lacking.

He also remembered every single favor, whether he was granting or receiving it, and acted like there was a ledger somewhere in which the value of each favor was calculated and a net sum—who now owed whom, and how much—was assessed.

About two-fifths of the Ellis empire's military contracts went through Marty Burgess's hands. That meant a lot of negotiations, and a lot of favors.

Well, maybe. It depended on who you asked.

"Max, you know we can't do that," Marty said.

They were on a regular voice call, because the U.S. government had yet to clear the Ellis Eyenets for official use. This was because Ellis Wearables refused to allow clients access to the security logging, which was considered proprietary. For some reason, there were people in the government who weren't comfortable taking their word for it that the Eyenet was secure.

"It's *important*, Marty," Max said. "I wouldn't ask otherwise. We think something might have happened to Sunset Station."

"We can't just re-task a satellite and you know it."

Pete brought the car to a stop at the edge of the tarmac. Up ahead, the flight crew was preparing the jet. Max muted the general. "I want to be in the air in ten," he said to Pete. "Tell them; I'll be there in a minute."

He unmuted Marty, as Pete got out of the car. "I think you *can*, Marty. I think you can tell one of the spy satellites using Ellis optics, Ellis digital, and Ellis networking, to take a *minute* out of its busy day of capturing top secret photos of the Russian president fucking a prostitute, to help us out. Or maybe, I don't know, maybe some of those top secret spy satellites, the ones *my space program helped you put up there*, suddenly aren't so top secret anymore."

"There's a process, Max," Marty said. "I'm not unsympathetic, but these things take time."

"How about this, Martin: whoever you have to talk to about it, tell them we think it was an attack."

"An... what *kind* of attack?"

"We think there's a real chance someone down here blew up my space station."

"That would take—"

"It would take rockets, fired from Earth. Rockets I'm guessing the Pentagon would want to know about, if they don't already."

There was a long enough pause that Max knew he had him. "You really think that?" Marty asked.

"I don't know what to think. None of us do. But we lost *all* contact, and I shouldn't have to explain how unlikely that is. We need images of the scene, and we can't wait."

"You're gonna owe me," Marty grumbled.

"I know," Max said.

"A lot."

"I *know*."

"I'll get back to you."

A HALF AN HOUR into the flight, Max's phone chirped with a text.

No launches detected. I need a secure maildrop.

It was from General Burgess's personal device.

Max pulled down a link to a private drop. If Marty had privacy or confidentiality concerns, Max could tell him the maildrop was at *least* as secure as what the Pentagon was using for its classified documents.

Marty didn't ask, though; he just sent through what he had.

Max tried to open the images on his phone, but they were too large, so he tried it on his laptop instead. As he did so, his phone rang.

"You got 'em?" Marty asked.

"I'm looking at them now, thanks."

There were three images, taken from a satellite coming at Sunset Station from the west, an angle where the ESS, the platform, and anything else up there would be captured in reflected sunlight.

They were all still there. Max could see three objects: the space platform, the ESS, and the shuttle.

That was the good news. The bad news was, none of the lights were on. Both the shuttle and the ESS had perimeter lighting, and the platform was supposed to have lights running along its edges. At least one set of lights should have been visible in the photos.

Space had suffered a power failure.

But, at least they were still there. That was something.

"Thanks, Martin," Max said. "I'll have the team in Monterrey comb through this; maybe we can figure out what happened."

"That's not why I needed the secure box, Max," Marty said. "And it's not why I called. Pull up the third image and look at it more closely."

Max did. Like the other two, it showed the same three objects. He zoomed in, moved around a bit, until...

"What *is* that?" he asked. "Is that an artifact of the camera?"

"It's your camera," the general said. "You tell us. But our guys don't think so. We're tasking another satellite to get a better look."

Back and behind Sunset Station, there was a region of space where it seemed like the stars themselves had become misaligned. They were still there, but (and this became more obvious when going between the second and third images) it was like they had been lifted and moved, as a group. There was even a demarcation point, a straight line where the disrupted space ended and the usual space began.

No, not just a line, he thought, as he traced it around the image. *A shape.*

There was something up there with them.

PAUL

THERE WERE no analog clocks on the shuttle. It wasn't something Paul had ever thought about before being stuck, adrift in space in a dead ship, wondering what time it was and how long they'd been working on a solution to the dead-and-adrift problem. He was pretty sure, if they survived this, the first thing he'd tell the ground to do was issue wristwatches to the team.

That was a pretty big "if" at this point.

Paul's only job, for the past however-long-it-had been, was to hand Davina what she asked for from the toolkit, report periodically on the lack of electrical power in the parts of the ship she couldn't see, and locate the spare oxygen tanks hidden in the floor.

The Earth was getting bigger in the window. All by itself, this wasn't a surprise; without power to keep them in a stable orbit, they were going to eventually get pulled into the gravity well of the largest local object. What was surprising was that it was happening fast enough for him to notice.

There would be a point after which, no amount of thruster power would suffice in getting them back to a stable orbit.

"How about now?" Davina asked. She was buried deep in the electronics that ran under the floor from the command console to various parts of the ship.

"Still dark," he said.

"Christ," she muttered. "Okay."

She extricated herself from the cabling, stood and stretched.

"One more place to check, and then we're done," she said.

"Done in what sense?"

"Done as in, it's over. I can't access the batteries directly unless we're in the dock; if the cutoff happened *at* that connection...?"

"Got it."

She looked outside for a long beat. "She's gone, isn't she? Kris is gone."

"We don't know that."

"Paul."

"For all we know, she's floating ten yards to our right, just out of view," he said. "Let's get the power back, and then we'll look."

He was being far more optimistic than was called for, and she knew it, but he could hardly have said anything else.

"Yes, all right," she said. "Come on, I need your help."

THEIR LAST SHOT at restoring power to the shuttle was in a floor panel at the back of the airlock.

The batteries lived on the other side of the airlock wall, next to the thrusters. Unlike with the space station, the shuttle had no solar panels for recharging its batteries. Instead, it connected to a charger directly, in the dock. (It was similar to how a lot of battery-powered devices recharged—Paul had a power drill at home that worked the same way—but it always struck him as a bonkers way to design a vehicle meant for space travel.) This was why they had no way to get to the battery contact points, in their quest for power restoration; the batteries were in the outer wall.

It was obvious Davina found what she was looking for as soon as they got the hatch opened.

"Do you hear that?" she asked, leaning closer to the cable connections beneath the panel door. "It's humming. There's power here."

"I hear it," he said.

It took another ten minutes of testing before she found the buffer that had stopped the power from flowing to the rest of the ship.

"Now's a good time for a prayer, if you're feeling religious," she said. Then she hit the reset button.

Nothing happened.

"No, no, no," Davina muttered.

Paul looked through the open door of the airlock, to the main chamber. Something on the front console was blinking.

"I think we're okay," he said. "We just have to hit the systems restart."

He drifted out of the airlock to the cockpit and into the chair, found the reset button and pushed it.

The lights came back on. So did about fifty alarms.

"*How can I help?*" Susie the Support Bot asked.

"Oh, hi, Susie," Paul said. "Weird as this may sound, it's good to hear your voice. What are all the alarms for?"

"Get out of the way," Davina said, grabbing Paul by the shoulder. "Go put the panel back and secure the airlock."

"Right," he said, stepping back.

"*Alarms go off when there's something wrong!*" Susie said.

"No shit, Susie," Davina said, her hands flying across the control panel. "We're sliding out of orbit."

ALAN

IT TOOK a while before Alan realized the screaming he was hearing wasn't the brake being applied anymore. It was Sandee. This realization came with the discovery that he was nearly weightless, and that getting to the ladder was no longer nigh-impossible, even in his current condition, which was: dying from CO_2 poisoning.

He pulled himself up into the now-much-wider tunnel leading to the main hub at the same time the screaming stopped, which was either a good sign or a very bad sign.

At the top, he found her jammed between the ladder and the wall. Her body was limp, but when he touched her, she snapped back awake.

"Are we dead? Are we dead?" she asked.

"It's Alan, and we're not dead."

"Alan? I can't feel my arms."

He ran his hand from her shoulders to her fingers. She'd jammed both of her hands between the brake and the rim of the airlock hatch, in order to force the brake arm open.

"You cut off the circulation," he said.

"They're still there?"

"Yes, your arms are still there. I think you can let go now."

"Are we stopped?" she asked.

"Nearly."

He put his ear up to the hatch, and listened. They were still spinning, but if he understood how this mechanism functioned...

There, he thought, as he heard a click. There was a gentle, directional tug, as the connection between the main hub and the tunnel was completed, and the spinning stopped completely.

"That's it," he said. "We're connected."

"Terrific. Help."

With some effort, he was able to get the brake locked into its original position, which freed up the arms she could neither move nor feel.

He needed Sandee to get out of the way so he could open the hatch, so he took her by the waist and tried to carry her partway down the ladder. Immediately, she screamed in pain.

"What?" he asked. "Your arms?"

"Fuuuuh...." she hissed. "My foot, it's... It's jammed in the ladder. Think it's broken."

He let go of her, pulled the light from his pocket, and shined it down her leg.

"Oh, man," he said.

"Tell me about it," she said, eyes closed and refusing to look.

"Do you want me to?"

"It's an expression. But yes. What are we talking about?"

"Yes, it's definitely broken," he said, which was the nicest way to say it. He wasn't sure the foot was even intact anymore. The minute she was freed from the ladder—it'd take a steel rod jammed between the rungs to force it open—there was a real chance of her bleeding out. "But I need to get the power back before we can do anything about it," he added. "Can I leave you?"

"To open this hatch? Hell, yes."

He climbed up next to her, found the wheel to the hatch, and braced himself as well as he could against the tunnel walls. It was slightly awkward, as he had to put his legs around the space occupied by Sandee's head.

"All right, here we go," he said, giving it a twist.

It took some work before he felt it give, and then spin freely. There was a loud hiss, as the air from the two spaces commingled. He pushed the hatch in.

The hub was dark and cold, but—and he was basing this on the fact that he didn't immediately die—intact. He climbed up and in. Then he floated in the middle of the hub for a few seconds, just enjoying the act of breathing. The taste of (relatively) fresh air was remarkable.

"How are we looking?" Sandee asked.

"I'll tell you in a minute," he said.

He went to the main console first. Josip told him it would be possible to reset the station's power either from the console, or the electrical panel by the batteries. "Whichever is flashing," he said.

There was exactly one button flashing on the console, for "main bus reset."

He pushed it. There was a loud *thump*, and then the lights kicked on, the air whooshed to life, and the control panel lit up in time with a dozen terrible-sounding alarms.

"How can I help?" Susie asked.

"Welcome back, Susie," Alan said. "I hope all these alarms can wait."

He headed back to the tunnel entrance.

"We're back," he said. "Let me get that foot free."

She looked up at him, pain all over her face. She still wasn't moving her arms, but hopefully this was just because the blood was returning and it hurt to move them, and not because of some kind of nerve damage. (They really needed Paul, who was the medical guy for this crew. That set Alan to wondering, for the first time in hours, how the shuttle crew was doing.)

"What the fuck are you talking about," she hissed through her teeth. "I'm fine; go get Josip out of that CO_2 well before it's too late."

DAVINA

DAVINA MANAGED to wrestle the shuttle out of the grip of the Earth's gravitational pull and back into a region of space in which it could safely operate without alarms going off. Her first task, as soon as that was complete, was to ping Kris.

Nothing.

She did a slow 360 next, then adjusted her vertical angle by 90 degrees and tried again. All she could really hope for was a visual, which she already knew was effectively an impossible prospect unless Kris was *very* nearby.

Babe, what happened to you? she thought. *Where did you go?*

She sent out another omnidirectional ping, and got nothing back, but rather than panic some more (which wasn't doing any good) she decided to interrogate how this could be.

All Davina was doing was sending out a pulse on the same frequency as the radio in Kris's helmet. The radio was supposed to, upon receipt, send one back. (It was meant to function without the astronaut's involvement, under the very reasonable assumption that there may be circumstances in which the astronaut was impaired in some way.) Dav should then be able to use the *direction* from which the ping came back at her to figure out where Kris was.

(It would have been fantastic if they had some sort of GPS technology in space, something that *always* knew precisely where everyone was. But global positioning satellite technology wasn't available to anyone not *on* the planet.)

No pingback could either mean the radio had been shorted out—just like everything aboard the shuttle—or was otherwise broken. Or it could mean Kris was out of range.

Davina didn't know what the range *was*, but figured it had to be a great distance. As in, Kris may well be alive somewhere out there, but officially too far away to be retrieved safely.

So hopefully, it wasn't that.

"Paul, can you look at the logs and work out how much air she has left?" she asked.

Paul was at another console, in the back half of the chamber. Their various communications links to the outside had been gradually awakening from a slumber, like a cat uncurling; as such, he was trying to contact the ESS.

"I'm waiting on the clocks to reset," he said. "I'll let you know as soon as I have it."

They did not know what time it was, which was just, just massively stupid. They were in a ship fixed to a discrete region of space relative to the planet beneath them; there was no, "later in the day," or, "twilight," or any of the signifiers of the passage of time. What they had was, the surface of the planet. But recognizing that the last time she looked down, they were above Korea, and now they were above northern Africa, didn't help as much as it should have, in part because Davina didn't actually know how long it took, from their current position, to *go* from the Korean peninsula to the Sahara.

All they had was the time being tracked by the clock in the computer... because Ellis Aerospace wanted everything to be run by computers—to the extent they promoted the lie that everything *was* run by computers—and failed to factor in a scenario in which *all* the computers failed.

Davina had a clock alarm back home that kept track of the time with a local battery in the event of a power outage. Somehow, nobody at Ellis thought that would be a useful function in their blessed spaceship.

Paul was waiting for the shuttle to reestablish a connection with one of the Ellis communications satellites, which would reset their clock. *Then, maybe*, they'd know if Kris was already dead.

The lack of a functioning timepiece wasn't what Davina found the most frustrating, though. Paul had already given up on Kris—she could hear it in his voice— but was letting Dav find her way there on her own. As much as she appreciated that he was motivated by good intentions, she *hated* being handled.

I know you're still out there, she thought. *I'll find you.*

"I've got the ESS!" Paul said. "They made it!"

"Great," Dav said. "They can help us look."

"Yeah, let me... give me a minute."

What followed was a lot of muttering, silence, and more muttering. They were talking about Kris. Obviously.

"Hang on, Alan," Paul said, louder. "I'm going to open the channel."

Paul, without asking, pushed the ESS audio to the whole shuttle.

"You've got both me and Davina, Alan," Paul said. "Can you repeat what you just said?"

"Hi Dav," Alan said. He sounded strained, like he was holding something heavy. "I'm sorry about—"

"What is it, Alan?" she asked, cutting him off. "I'm busy with the search. We're down one out here, if Paul didn't tell you."

"He did. He did. Ah. We're in a bad way over here. Sandee... we think she may lose her foot, and I haven't been able to revive Josip. I have him on oxygen. Sandee's on pain meds, and I'm having trouble slowing the bleeding. We need Paul, ASAP."

"We have to find Kris," she said. "I'm not giving up on her."

"I understand that, but I also don't want to risk losing two to look for someone who..." he sighed. "You know what I'm saying. I don't want to *order* you back, Dav."

"I understand that if we let Kris die, you will end up in charge, and that presumptively *ordering* me to allow that to happen guarantees your order has followed the correct chain of command."

"It's not like that, Davina," Paul said. "You know that."

A tear welled up in Dav's eye that she brushed away. They weren't allowed to see her cry. She looked at Paul. "Find out how much time she has left," she said. "Give me at least that much. I don't want to go back before I'm sure."

"Alan?" Paul said.

"Okay," Alan said. "Take the time. Davina, I hope she's okay. You know I do."

Davina nodded silently, and tried another sweep.

Show me something, Kris, she thought. *Please.*

KRIS

"HOW CAN I HELP?"

Kris blinked her eyes open to a singular view of the galaxy. Stars, everywhere. No sun, or Earth, or moon. Just stars.

"Is that you, asshat?" she asked.

"How can I help?" Susie repeated.

"I don't know yet."

"Of course!"

It was a waste of time to ask herself where she *was*, because that much was obvious: she was in space. Somewhere. The fact that she couldn't *see* the sun, Earth or moon had to mean she was facing the wrong way, rather than that she was currently too far away from them. She couldn't remember exactly how she'd ended up in this situation, but felt confident that however she *got* to this nondescript part of space, she'd traveled to it via ordinary means.

She held up one hand and noted the back of it was lit up; the sun was definitely behind her.

So, where is the Earth?

She tried to turn her head, and when that didn't yield the

desired results, she tried activating the thrusters built into the suit, to help spin her around.

They weren't working.

"Asshat? Susie, I mean," she said.

"How can I help?"

"Can you tell me why my thrusters aren't working?"

"I don't know the answer to that!" Susie said.

About half the time, when Susie didn't know something, she would try to help by looking up possible answers on the internet, or the ESS's database. That she didn't do this probably meant Kris was talking to the local version of Susie the Support Bot.

Not that Kris needed any confirmation that her current situation was *dire*, but the fact that this Susie wasn't in contact with the ESS's version of Susie? Was bad.

What happened *to me?* Kris wondered.

She remembered being on her way to the shuttle, seeing Davina in the window, and then there was... there was some kind of feedback on the radio, and then...?

Then I blacked out.

That was the order of events, but they didn't make sense.

The story was missing something; something between looking at Davina, and the moment when she was hit with the feedback. What was it? And how did any of that cause her to black out, never mind sending her adrift?

Space folded, she thought. *I saw space fold, and...?*

She had this sense that something else happened, before the blackout, that she should be remembering. It was possibly very important, this something; more important than "space folding," which was definitely not a normal function of space.

She just had to remember what it was.

"No, Kris," she said to herself. "It's not important. Solve for what's in front of you, worry about the rest later."

"*How can I help?*" Susie asked.

"Shut up, asshat," Kris said.

"*Of course!*"

"Actually, I take that back. Susie?"

"*How can I help?*"

"Am I moving?" Kris asked.

"*I don't know the answer to that!*" Susie said.

"Yeah, sorry, I guess you wouldn't," Kris said, sighing.

"*Relative to what?*"

Susie had never asked a follow-up before; this was new. "Say again?" Kris asked.

"*Are you moving, relative to what?*" Susie clarified.

That was a really good question.

"I'll rephrase," Kris said. "Am I moving, relative to the ESS?"

"*Yes! Relative to the Ellis Space Station, you are moving.*"

"Thank you, Susie," Kris said. "Do you know how *fast* I'm moving? In kilometers per hour."

"*Your current rate is 1.87 kilometers per hour, relative to the Ellis Space Station.*"

"Thank you, Susie. You're being very helpful."

"*Of course!*"

"I'm sorry I called you asshat."

"*Of course!*"

Wait a minute, she thought. *How does she know that?*

"Susie, are you in communication with Sunset Station?"

"*How can I help?*"

Kris sighed. There were rules, when talking to Susie.

"Are you in communication with Sunset Station?" Kris repeated.

"*I don't understand the question!*"

"You provided my speed relative to the ESS. Do you know where the ESS is?"

"The Ellis Space Station is 6.19 kilometers from your current location, and moving away at a rate of 1.87 kilometers per hour," Susie said.

Kris nearly asked if the *station* was moving, or if *she* was moving, before reminding herself that this was a useless question: 1.87 was their velocity relative to one another, period. They would need a third object to discuss who was doing all the moving, and even then, the question didn't necessarily make sense.

Assuming Susie was correct about any of this—Kris very definitely didn't *want* to assume any facts from asshat were correct, but she had little choice here—Kris had been separated from the Sunset Station region of space for over three hours.

She didn't know how much oxygen she had left, but it couldn't be a whole hell of a lot. The problem there was, much like her thrusters, the onboard system that logged and reported her oxygen levels appeared to be offline.

"Susie," Kris said, remembering to pause this time.

"How can I help?"

"Can you tell me how much more oxygen I have left?"

"I don't understand the question!"

"Right. Okay. Um, new question. If I needed to *stop* my velocity, relative to the ESS, can you tell me in which direction I should apply thrust?"

Susie didn't answer right away, which was alarming. In a *human*, Kris would interpret this to mean she was thinking about it. But Susie never thought about anything, because Susie didn't actually *think*.

"I can't do that!" Susie said, finally.

"Why not?" Kris asked. "Since you seem to know where the ESS is."

"Directions would require precise angular measurements against established points of reference!"

She needed to give Kris something to aim *for*, in other words. This made perfect sense. Which, again, was not a normal characteristic of Susie the Support Bot.

Kris said, "How about, second star to the left, and straight on 'til morning? Would that work?"

"*I don't understand those points of reference!*"

"Sorry, ignore that."

"*Of course!*"

"Susie?"

"*How can I help?*"

"I would like to get back to Sunset Station. Can you tell me *roughly* what direction in which to apply thrust, and then provide me with adjustments along the way? Is that something you can do?"

"*I can't do that!*" Susie said. "*Kris Standard's thrusters are not responding!*"

"Pretend they are for a sec," Kris said. She had no idea if Susie was capable of rumination on a hypothetical, but what the hell. "If I *did* have a way to apply thrust, would you be able to do as I asked?"

Susie thought about it some more.

"*I can do that!*" Susie said. "*Please answer: how will you apply thrust?*"

"Well?" Kris said, as she confirmed that the toolkit was still attached to her belt. "Let's just say this is the least favorite part of my plan."

MORRIS

A CHEER WENT UP in the control room when Alan Blanken checked in.

Morris wasn't on the floor when it happened; he was in the visitors' viewing section, talking to Max Ellis, who had already been there for an hour, along with two of his assistants and a local-hire bodyguard, present to make sure nobody in Mexico decided to kidnap a billionaire today.

Max had sent ahead some images showing that Sunset Station was still where it was supposed to be. They had no evident power—which didn't make sense—but they were there.

To everyone else, this meant they'd probably just lost six people, because space isn't the kind of place humans can live without power for long periods. And it meant the same thing to Max Ellis, but it *also* meant... well, that wasn't entirely clear, but he seemed pretty excited about something in one of the images.

Morris, and about half of his team, had looked at the same images; they all agreed the thing that had Max all excited wasn't anything more than a glitch in the digital photograph. The head of optics even offered to reproduce the effect, if anyone was interested.

Max didn't care for this explanation, and as a counterpoint told them that the source of the satellite images *also* thought they were seeing evidence of something else up there, lurking behind Sunset Station in a curtain of stars. Max declined to say who that source was (presumably someone in the U.S. military apparatus) which somewhat damaged the weight of the citation, but that didn't ultimately matter, because Max Ellis didn't have to *convince* anyone on the Monterrey team of anything; he already owned the company. If he said there was something there, they had to pretend there was, and act accordingly.

Morris thought this was Max's way of coping with a total catastrophe, and was in the middle of was trying to find a polite way to say that exact thing, when he heard the cheer. He ran back to the control room.

"Glad to hear from you, Alan!" Adrian was saying. She saw Mo run in and gave him a thumbs-up. "You guys gave us a scare. How's everyone doing up there?"

"Not fantastic," Alan said, over a decent amount of static. "The shuttle's docking now. We have to get Paul into the hub to help with Sandee and Josip."

Morris grabbed a free headset and nodded an *I'm jumping in* to Adrian. "Alan, this is Mo," he said. "Sandee and Josip?"

"I think Jo might be okay," Alan said. "He was trying to find oxygen tanks in the Habitat floor and... it's a long story, but he basically stuck his face in a layer of CO_2 and didn't come back up. But he's breathing okay now, and he just opened his eyes. Sandee... her foot was crushed pretty bad."

"Her foot?" Mo asked. "How?"

"That's another long story. I knocked her out with some meds. But like I said, we're getting Paul aboard ASAP; we'll know better in a bit. You guys have medical in the room? Pretty sure he'll need a consult."

"Darius is here," Morris said. "He'll be ready. How are Davina and Kris?"

"Davina's fine; she's going to drop Paul off and head back out. We think we lost Kris."

This killed the mood in the control room pretty quickly.

"Understood," Mo said. "*Why* is Davina heading back out?"

"She wants to keep looking," Alan said. "We don't know what we experienced up here, but Kris was free walking when it happened, and the shuttle lost sight of her. By our calculations, Kris has about, ah... yeah, about forty minutes of air left. *Optimally*. Think Dav plans to keep looking for her until then. I had to *order* her to bring Paul in, Mo. I'm not going to tell her she can't go back out. I know it's a risk."

"Until we know what happened, it's a huge risk," Morris said. "But I understand. Keep us in the loop."

Max manifested in the space to Morris's left. "Let me talk to him."

"It's not, uh," *protocol,* was the rest of Mo's sentence. There were some people authorized to speak to the astronauts and some who were not, and the reason was that there were certain things one just didn't say, and those certain things were not necessarily intuitive. There was an entire certification program, which Max Ellis had not, in all likelihood, participated in.

But, it was Max; he got to talk to the astronauts if he wanted to. Morris handed over the headset.

"Alan, this is Max Ellis," Max said.

"Oh, hello, Mr. Ellis," Alan said. "Sorry if we broke your space platform. It's been a busy 24."

Max looked like he'd forgotten all about the space platform. "Oh," he said. "That's okay. Is it... is it still up there? We have images..."

"It is, sir, but the lattice hasn't restarted on its own, and we're not in a position to reach it right now. We'll let you know if a flight to repair is feasible before it reaches the point of no return. Right now, we have different priorities."

"I understand," Max said. His expression said he no longer gave a damn about the platform, which was actually good news; Morris wasn't about to send someone back out there if he could avoid doing so. "Listen, can you look to your right, and tell me what you see?"

"Uh."

"Outside. Not in the cockpit. I mean to the right of the ESS."

There was a pause, as Alan (presumably) leaned forward and looked.

"Lots of stars?" Alan said. "Not sure I understand the ask, Mr. Ellis. Is this, are you reaching for some kind of metaphor, or...?"

Morris hit the mute button on Max's end of the conversation. "Max," he said. "I know you're eager to check this out, but half the team is either missing or seriously injured. This is not the time."

For perhaps a quarter of a second, it looked like Max was going to fire Mo on the spot. Then he nodded, and handed the headset back. "You're right," he said. "We have time." He looked at one of his assistants—her name was a mystery to all—and said, "stay here. I want updates every twenty minutes."

Then he marched out.

Morris unmuted the line. "Sorry, Alan," he said. "Mr. Ellis had to run."

"What was that about?" Alan asked.

"I'll explain later. Give us an update on Jo and Sandee, and then we'll talk you through getting the rest of the station up and running."

"Sounds good, M—holy shit!"

"What? What is it?"

Alan cut off the call at his end, leaving everyone in mission control confused and looking at each other.

"Did he hang up on us?" Morris asked. "Or did we lose the station again?"

DAVINA

"DAVINA, how close are you to getting back out there?" Alan asked, over the comms. There was some degree of urgency in his voice.

Davina was in the shuttle cockpit, in the station's front dock, and about ten minutes from departure, provided the shuttle could figure out how to stop being so stubborn. It had never been taken back out immediately upon docking, and was busy running through its usual maintenance and recharge cycles with the leisure of someone who didn't expect to be bothered for the rest of the day.

"I'm running the final systems check and getting back out there, Alan," she said. "You're not going to order me to stay now, are you? Because I will not comply. I don't care what Monterrey told you."

"Dav, Kris just flew past the window," he said. "I'm turning the station to keep her in view, but I don't think you have a lot of time."

━━━

ELLIS AERO'S shuttle was a piece of crap. Everybody who'd attempted to pilot it agreed on this basic point.

There was one proper thrust engine at the tail of the craft. It provided overmuch forward momentum in contrast to the ten attitude thrusters positioned at various points around the hull. The strength of the tail thruster was not adequately offset by the collective strength of the attitude thrusters—which sometimes had to act as brakes, only they couldn't really do that without a substantial runway.

In short, it was very easy to accidentally run the shuttle into whatever solid object happened to be nearby, even when given several minutes to correct for the mistake, because the attitude thrusters weren't up to the task.

They also were not great at adjusting the ship's pitch, roll and yaw, which was only their primary function. They tended to misfire at inappropriate moments, sending the shuttle into an unanticipated barrel roll or flat spin, which could be correctable in open space, but really dangerous in tight maneuvering situations, such as when docking.

The way to pilot the shuttle from place to place was to either goose the main engine into a gentle forward momentum—which meant positively *crawling* from one place to the next—or to push ahead more aggressively, turn the shuttle 180 degrees with the attitude thrusters (with tiny bursts, in case of a misfire) and fire the main engine again.

The second method was the one preferred by the ground crew, for its speed. For anyone who actually had to *pilot* the damned thing, the first method was both less stressful and less risky. It just took longer.

None of them had ever attempted to push the shuttle's main thruster to anything close to full capacity before. But when Davina pulled away from the ESS, oriented the shuttle in line with the station's twelve o'clock, and got her first glimpse of Kris in rapid retreat, she realized that nothing less than full would do.

Get to her first, she thought. *Work out the rest after.*

She tweaked the angle using a sighting matrix projected by the ship's computer on the dome window. She wanted to come up alongside of Kris; a bad initial angle would make that just about impossible.

Once she was satisfied she had the right coordinates, she pushed the throttle down. The shuttle rocketed forward, the inertial force shoving her backward in the chair.

"Too fast, too fast," she muttered, adjusting the attitude thrusters to full reverse (as in, facing directly backwards) and firing them to bleed off a *little* of the momentum.

"*How can I help?*" Susie asked.

"Not now, Susie."

"*Of course!*"

"Alan, is Kris talking at all?" Davina asked.

"I've been trying to get a response," he said. "I think her suit's probably shorted, just like everything else was."

"Then how is she...? Oh, I see."

Still more than a hundred yards out, Davina was close enough to see that Kris had the hose of an oxygen tank wrapped around one of her mitts, with the tank itself on her chest.

"Alan, I think she popped a pinhole in one of her oxy tank hoses, for thrust," Davina said. "She may have already run out of oxygen."

"Understood," he said. "Not much we can do about that right now."

Fifty-odd yards out, it looked like the shuttle was going to come within about fifteen feet of Kris on its way by, which was simultaneously a happy confirmation that the initial angle calculations were almost perfect, and a disappointment that she hadn't gotten any closer.

She passed Kris on the left, allowed the shuttle to get another fifty yards ahead and then flipped the ship nose-over-tail 180 degrees, putting her in an "upside-down" orientation compared to her prior position, while keeping the airlock on the correct side of the ship. Then she goosed the main thruster for a while, until she was satisfied that she and Kris were traveling at approximately the same velocity.

"All right," Dav said, taking a deep breath to steady her nerves. "I can do this."

She engaged the attitude thrusters, to nose up closer to Kris. Immediately, one of the little sons-of-bitches misfired, and would have rolled her over had she not caught it and offset.

Steady, steady…

At twenty yards, she cycled the atmosphere out of the airlock and opened the airlock door.

"Susie?"

"*How can I help?*" Susie asked.

For no plausible reason she could think of, the shuttle's designers had neglected to include cameras on the starboard or port sides of the shuttle. There was one on the tail, another on the roof and a third on the underside, but she couldn't use any of those to see the outside of the airlock. There was a camera *in* the airlock, but it offered only a partial, angled view of the outside; it was really there to show the interior.

"In about ten seconds, I'm going to lose sight of Kris," Davina said. "Can you help me catch her in the airlock?"

"*Kris Standard is not aboard the shuttle,*" Susie said.

"I know this. She's outside. Can you see her?"

"*I don't understand! Can you rephrase?*"

Goddammit. "No, forget it. I'll do this blind."

"*The leading causes of blindness, according to…*"

"Shut up, Susie."

"*Of course!*"

She tweaked the shuttle to within a few feet of Kris, close enough that if she could open a window, she'd be able to reach out and grab her.

Then Kris passed out of view. As soon as that happened, Davina fired the thrusters to turn the shuttle sideways, and into Kris's path. If it went right, she'd catch Kris inside the airlock. If it went *wrong*, Kris would bounce off the hull and on a new trajectory, and Dav would have to do this all over again.

She brought the airlock camera up on her main screen, and began to pray.

KRIS

KRIS WOKE up in the ESS common room, strapped to a cot and breathing oxygen through a mask, confused as to how she got there.

Waking up lashed to something could be an alarming experience, but she'd been sleeping in a bundled sleeping bag for so long that the sensation of being restricted was, weirdly, somewhat comforting. Somebody else did this to her, but that somebody was trying to take care of her, so it was okay.

There was a tube attached to her arm, connected to a device that was designed to deliver intravenous fluids without needing gravity. (IV drips in space didn't drip.) It didn't look like blood, could have been plasma, but was probably food.

What happened to me? she wondered.

Sandee was there too, on her own cot. She had a *bunch* of IVs, and an air cast on her leg.

What happened to her?

Clearly, Kris had missed a couple of things.

She tilted her head to get a look at the other side of the room, and discovered Davina, belted into a chair and sleeping.

"Dav," Kris said. Her mouth was dry and she was talking

through a mask; her voice was barely audible. She tried again, louder. "Dav. Hey."

Davina stirred, went through a quarter second of panic, as she tried to figure out where she was and why she was floating, then found Kris, and smiled. "You're back," she said.

Dav slipped the mask off of Kris's face and kissed her.

"I'm back," Kris agreed. She couldn't exactly recall where she'd *been,* but she was definitely back. "Can I have some water?"

She could not have water, but she could have ice chips. While Davina crossed the room to get her some, Josip poked his head in.

"Ah, good, I see you are awake," he said. "We could use another hand."

"It's nice to see you too," she said. Davina floated back into Kris's limited view.

"Ignore him," Dav said. "Carbon dioxide killed all the brain cells that made him tolerable."

Jo laughed. To Kris, he said, "did she tell you how you got here?"

"*Just* woke up," Kris said. "I only figured out where *here* is a minute ago."

"The most amazing maneuver ever conducted is how," Jo said. "They will be talking about it for many years."

"Josip, go fix something," Davina said. "She needs her rest."

Jo shook a wrench at the two of them. "Yes, rest. More American laziness, when there are things to do."

He left before Davina could curse him out appropriately.

"He knows I'm Canadian, right?" Kris asked.

"I don't think he knows the difference."

"What was that about amazing maneuvers?"

"Oh," Davina said, "that." She was embarrassed, somehow.

Davina never got embarrassed, so this was new. "I had to catch you with the shuttle. It's nothing."

"Why did you have to...? Oh. Oh, God."

"What is it?"

"Nothing, I just remembered... Waking up in deep space, with no idea... Dav, no way I should still be alive."

"Yes, dear," Davina said. "We know."

———

PAUL CHECKED on her a few minutes later. He asked Davina to step out so he could perform a cognitive test, which, he said, required privacy. (This wasn't true; the truth was, he was worried that Dav would tip her off on the answers if she struggled. Kris thought this was a perfectly valid concern.)

She passed the cognitive test, and was healthy enough to come off the IV fluids, so he unhooked all the stuff, unstrapped her from the cot, helped her sit up, and got her the drink of water she was so craving. *Then*—and this was another reason not to have Davina in the room—he told Kris precisely how close she'd come to dying.

"We're estimating that you'd run out of oxygen about a minute before Davina caught you," he said. "Not sure when you lost consciousness, but I guess that was a kindness. How much do you remember?"

"I remember using a laser cutter to pop a hole in one of my hoses," she said. "It was the only way to get back here, since my thrusters were broken."

Paul gave her one of those non-expression expressions, where he's obviously trying to *not* react non-verbally, to the extent that it becomes a reaction all its own. He was really good at it, but she knew him about as intimately as it was possible to know a person without being in a relationship with them, so she caught it.

"Uh-huh," he said blankly. "Did Davina tell you anything about what happened around here?"

"She said everyone lost power," Kris said.

"That's right," he said. "*Before* the power loss, when you were on your way back to the shuttle: do you remember anything happening?"

"Not really, no," she said.

"You said you saw something. Before you were cut off. No idea what that was?"

Space folding, she thought. *And then something else that I can't describe, thanks for reminding me.* Kris wasn't ready to talk about any of that yet, because she didn't think she'd make any sense if she tried, and didn't want to *not* make sense to someone who had just finished testing her for cognitive impairment.

"I'm sorry, I don't," she said. "What caused the outage?"

"We're still trying to work that out," he said. "Ground thinks it was some kind of EMP, which somewhat fits the evidence, but, well, that's not my area. It knocked out the power in Sunset Station: the shuttle, the ESS, the platform. But it didn't *push* any of us into a new vector. Whereas with you..."

"I was sent on a tour of the galaxy, I know," she said. "I can't explain how that happened any more than you can, Paul. Maybe I inadvertently activated one of my thrusters before they broke on me."

Paul nodded. "There's a lot we still don't understand," he said. "How did you know which direction?"

"What do you mean?"

"When you opened the hose on your tank to make it back here. How did you know which way to aim yourself? Because you came within a hundred yards of the ESS; that's... that's pretty incredible."

Kris laughed. "It's a little embarrassing," she said.

"Okay...?"

"It was Susie."

"Susie," he repeated.

"She knew the right vector. After all the shit I've given her for not being helpful at *all*, she ended up saving my life."

"*How can I help?*" Susie said.

"We're fine, Susie, thank you," Kris said.

"*Of course!*"

"So yeah," Kris said. "Embarrassing. Guess I have to stop calling her asshat."

———

KRIS WAS ORDERED BY PAUL, in his capacity as station doctor, to go to her private bunk and rest, which she promised to do as soon as she got an update on everything going on with the ship.

"Alan has the reins," Paul said. "He'll be fine to cover for you until you're ready to return to your duties."

"What I'm hearing is, you don't think I'm ready to return to my duties yet."

"I'll let you know," he said, smiling.

There was definitely something he wasn't telling her, but whatever. He was right that she wasn't ready to jump in and run things, but part of the reason why, was that she didn't know what the *state* of anything was. She was aware that they nearly lost Josip and Sandee, and the space platform had either been sucked into Earth orbit or was about to be, and all of this was because of a mysterious power something-something that nobody understood and was potentially an *attack* of some kind.

But she didn't know where things were *now*.

For that, she needed to be on the bridge, so rather than head straight to her room, she went there instead.

Alan was at the console. He had a headset on, and appeared to be in the middle of a conference call with a dozen people.

He saw her come in, waved, and said, "hey guys, I have to jump," as if this was a normal business meeting instead of a communication with a guy in orbit.

(She knew these calls; she'd been on many herself. Command had a bureaucratic component that was about 75% pointless, 20% wrong, and 5% useful, and there was no way to tell which way it was going to go ahead of time.)

"Welcome back," he said, taking off the headset.

"Thanks. How are you enjoying command?"

"Right now? It's a nightmare," he said. "But I'm under orders not to give you too many details, so that's all you're getting."

She laughed. "Of course you are. How about the highlights? Does Max Ellis want us to risk life and limb to recover his precious space platform?"

"He does indeed. And that's only one of the bugs up his ass. We're working on something to get it back, but it would be nice to know what *happened* to take us all out of commission first. And, we're down one until further notice. You saw Sandee?"

"Yeah, that's awful."

"The bucket's lateral motion would have torn the station apart eventually," he said. "She saved all of us, in exchange for her foot."

"Is she going to lose it?" Kris asked.

"I don't think anyone knows. I'm pushing to have her rotated back down ASAP, but we'll see. Might not matter."

They problem was that broken bones didn't heal well in zero gravity. And if what Davina told Kris was right, basically every bone in Sandee's right foot was broken. Even if Sandee was on *Earth*, she might not ever heal completely. In space, the odds were much worse.

"Then there's you," Alan said.

"Then there's me."

"I take it Paul already told you how dead you're supposed to be now."

"He might have," she said.

"Oh, hey, do you want to see Dav's maneuver? I assume she told you."

"Um, sure," Kris said, although Davina hadn't told her anything about it. "Yes, I'd love to."

Alan pulled up a recording made from one of the station's external cameras, and put it on the nearest screen.

"So here's you," he said, pointing to Kris in her spacesuit, sailing off into the wherever, oxy tank on her chest and all.

This was... unnerving.

"That you made it this far is astonishing," he said. "And really lucky. I happened to be looking out the window when you flew past; if I hadn't been, we never would've seen you."

"I asked Susie to connect with the station as soon as we were in range," she said. "I take it she didn't do that?"

Alan laughed; he evidently thought she was kidding. Kris didn't know why he thought that, but didn't probe any further, because then something *insane* happened on the video screen.

The shuttle zoomed into view, caught up with unconscious Kris, passed her, flipped upside-down, got next to her, turned 90 degrees, and caught her in the open airlock, like a ballplayer scooping up a ground ball.

Kris gasped. It probably didn't look all that amazing to anyone unfamiliar with the Ellis shuttle's limitations, but for someone who had struggled at the controls to get it to do *anything* involving precision and timing, it was simply absurd.

"There's a small army of aeronautical engineers who want to interview her about this," Paul said.

"She said no?" Kris asked.

"She said she's busy."

Kris laughed. "We're all busy. Speaking of, I should follow doctor's orders and get some more rest, seeing as how everyone thinks I should be dead. But when I get back, I want a full rundown."

"As soon as Paul clears you."

Before she made it all the way out of the bridge, something he'd said earlier came back to her. "Hey," she said. "What was the other bug?"

"The other what?"

"Up Max's ass. What was the other bug?"

"Oh," Alan said, laughing. "I actually think he has like ten of them up there, but he's got us on a snipe hunt for, well, I don't know what he *thinks* it is, but whatever; it's not there. I've been putting him off, because we have *actual* work to do."

"Tell me more?" she asked.

"Really?"

"Yeah, I want to know."

"It's, okay, he had NASA, or the military, or someone, get a satellite image of Sunset Station while we were down. I'll show you."

Alan pushed a still image to one of the screens, showing the three Ellis properties dead in the proverbial water. "He and some other people who've spent too much time staring at the bottom of a beer glass think they see something *here*."

Alan traced out an area on the image.

It definitely did look peculiar, like that part of space was misaligned.

"Optical artifact," Kris said.

"That's what I keep telling them. I don't know why, but Mr. Ellis doesn't want to listen."

"Yeah, well... he doesn't get to hear 'no' all that often," she said, looking more closely at the image.

Folded space, she thought.

"So where is this nonexistent object?" she asked.

"Supposedly, right here," Alan said, pointing to the grand vista of empty space before them.

"Have you gone looking for it?"

"Looking for what?" He asked. "You see the great big nothing I see, right?"

"Yeah. Yeah, I do... How are we doing for drones?"

"Uh. We still have the one, I believe."

The drones were in constant need of repair. The mission began with four, but one lost communication with the station in the middle of a maneuver and was now enthusiastically orbiting Venus, and another collapsed into its component parts ten seconds after hitting the vacuum of space, for no obvious reason.

Of the remaining drones, one had a faulty gyroscope that could be repaired with parts available on the station; they just hadn't found the time yet to take care of it. That left them with the one.

"Send it out," she said.

"You're serious."

"Why not? It's low risk. Have Davina pilot it. Aim for that region of space, and if it doesn't *hit* anything, you've still made Max happy."

"I kind of enjoy saying no to him," he said.

"Totally fair," she said. "Not the best career strategy, but totally fair."

KRIS WENT to her bunk after that, and actually slept. She dreamed of being lost in the middle of space again, only this time instead of Susie, she had her mother's voice in her ear. Naturally, her mother didn't listen to anything Kris was saying, and blamed her for the predicament she was in. Then she heard a terrible hissing noise, her helmet glass fractured, and... she woke up.

No more of that, thanks, she thought, as she extricated herself from the bag.

There was a knock on the folding plastic door.

(They didn't get blast doors on their rooms, never mind the nifty sliding metal doors everyone gets in sci-fi movies, although there were multiple depictions of the interior of the ESS floating around the internet that showed otherwise.)

Happy for the company, Kris accordioned the plastic to one side. Paul was there, with his worried face on.

"Can we talk?" he asked.

"Love to," she said. "Can I get some coffee first?"

He pulled his hand down from the other side of the doorway. It was holding a coffee.

"You *are* a good doctor," she said. "Did I ever tell you that?"

"I'm barely a doctor at all," he said, which was true. Professionally speaking, he was actually a nurse, but he was the closest thing they had to a medical expert aboard, so he may as well be one.

She took the coffee. "What's on your mind?" she asked.

He stepped in and shut the door, an act that was basically an extension of his serious face.

"I was just at the airlock with Josip," he said. "We were giving your suit a once-over. The, um, the surge, or whatever it was. We're calling it the surge. It knocked out all the computers in the shuttle and the station."

"I know."

"It also took out the computer in your suit. That's why you had no thrusters, and why you couldn't ping back Davina."

"Okay," she said. "I'm not getting the point."

"Kris, Susie couldn't have helped you find your way back here," he said.

"Except she did, Paul. I couldn't have done that calculation myself. Maybe, maybe the part of the computer, her part, wasn't damaged. That has to be it, right?"

Paul nodded. "We checked that," he said. "The whole thing's fried, Kris. We can't get it working *now*. All you had out there was basic life support."

"I calculated the right vector *myself*, is that what you're telling me? And, and the person my unconscious decided to manifest, in *that* moment, was Susie the asshat bot? Does that really sound like me?"

"I'm only telling you what I know," he said. "Susie wasn't available; your making it back here, it *had* to be luck. Unless..."

"Unless my whole story is bullshit," she said.

"I'm not accusing you of anything. But I do think we should hold off on clearing you"

"What, until I make up a better story? You're not benching me, Paul."

"I just want to put a pause..."

The room intercom whistled then. Good timing. She opened the line. "Go ahead," she said.

"Hey, Kris," Alan said. "I've got the drone outside and Davina helming. Thought you'd want to be here."

"Yes, Alan," she said, staring at Paul. "I really do want to be on the bridge right now. Thank you. Give me one minute."

She opened the room door. "We'll talk about this again later," she said, and stormed out.

(It was actually not possible to storm out of a room in zero gravity. She *floated* out, which was an incredibly ineffective way to depart with purpose.)

Kris was at the bridge a minute later.

"How are you feeling?" Dav asked, without turning. She was manipulating the controls of the drone, and watching the first-person feed on one of the screens.

"Super-fantastic," Kris said.

"Thanks for coming," Alan said. "Drone's deployed. What do you want us to do with it?"

"I don't know yet," Kris said, looking at the open space in her direct line of vision.

"I could just drive the drone straight ahead," Davina said. "If there's something solid out there, we would know it rather quickly."

"But it's our only working drone," Kris said. "Let's, hmm. Let's assume Max is right for a second, and there's an object hiding in that region of space. What would be the least invasive way to confirm it?"

"We could fire the yardstick," Alan offered.

"Yes," Kris said, "we could fire the yardstick. That's perfect. Try it."

The yardstick was a sighting laser. It measured distances by bouncing a laser off solid, flat surfaces, and figuring its distance from the object based on how long it took the beam to bounce back. It had an extremely limited use—the laser didn't come right back when hitting an angled surface—but (importantly) it was a tool that was currently attached to the drone.

Davina fired the laser. After about five seconds, she said, "That beam is heading for Jupiter now. Next?"

"Change the plane and try again," Kris said.

Davina did, and got the same result, moved the drone a third time and tried once more. Then a fourth, and a fifth.

On the sixth try, something absurd happened: the beam bounced back.

"Oh," Davina said.

"What?" Kris asked.

"It's saying there's something out there. Twelve hundred yards and change."

Alan looked out the window. "Do it again," he said.

They could see the drone in the window, but not the laser it was firing, which was disappointing but not a surprise. But they could also see that there remained nothing out there for the laser to bounce off of.

"Same result," Davina said, after a beat.

"This is really strange," Kris said.

"Hang on," Alan said. "Something's happening."

Then space *folded* again.

Kris gasped.

"Everyone's seeing that, right?" she asked.

"We are," Dav said.

When space finished churning, it was as if a curtain holding stars had dropped away, revealing... something that wasn't supposed to be there.

That's what I saw, Kris realized.

It was silver-gray, with smooth, rounded contours, and no visible windows or openings, shaped somewhat like a tadpole. The fattest part of the ship—the head, in tadpole physiology—had two round cylinders jutting out of the "chin." They looked like weapons.

"Holy shit," Davina said. "Is that...?"

"It is," Kris said. "It's an alien spaceship."

"Guys," Alan said, "It looks like our mission just changed."

"How can I help?" Susie asked.

ABOUT THE AUTHOR

Gene Doucette is the author of over twenty sci-fi/fantasy titles, including the Sorrow Falls series (*The Spaceship Next Door, The Frequency of Aliens,* and *Graffiti on the Wall of the Universe*), the Immortal series, *Fixer* and *Fixer Redux,* the *Tandemstar* books, and *The Apocalypse Seven.* Gene lives in Cambridge, MA.

For the latest on Gene Doucette, follow him online
genedoucette.me
genedoucette@me.com